IMAGE *adjuster*

LILY ALEXANDER

Image Adjuster

Copyright © 2020 by Lily Alexander

This book is a work of fiction. Names, characters, businesses, places, events, locales, and incidents are either the products of the author's imagination or used in a fictitious manner. Any resemblance to actual persons, living or dead, or actual events is purely coincidental.

ISBN: 978-1-7345686-0-8 (Ebook)
ISBN: 978-1-7345686-2-2 (Paperback)

Cover Design: Kate Farlow, Y'all. That Graphic.
Interior Design: Stephanie Anderson, Alt 19 Creative

ALSO BY
Lily Alexander

Image Protector

For my beloved husband.
Thank you for continuing to tell me I could,
and I should, and I already had.
I promise it won't take a decade for the next one!

CHAPTER

SEEING OLLIE PARKINSON hanging over the edge of a canyon by his ankle on the wrong side of the guard rail should have made Stephanie nervous, but she was still far too angry.

Instead, she was slightly amused and honestly pretty impressed by her bodyguard Alan's strength. His seemingly immovable confidence that he wasn't going to drop the actor on his head into the rocky hill below was just an extra layer of interesting.

Maybe it wasn't confidence at all actually; maybe he didn't care if that happened. She didn't mind either way at the moment.

"Come on you bitch! Is this really necessary? You assaulted me with your shoe in the car! I'll sue!" Ollie kept reaching for the guardrail and trying to pull himself up as he cursed at both her and Alan. It didn't seem like a wise strategy honestly, but all they could do was watch him wriggle like a worm on a hook. He almost managed to get his hands around Alan's arm to use as a pull-up bar, but Alan slapped him away and gave a good shake, making Ollie yell.

Stephanie's hackles rose way up at the slur he tossed her way, her long brown hair blowing irritatingly into her face. She knew she should have worn it up instead of loose.

"You hired this *bitch*, for the record. Because you need a boost after you went viral for all the wrong reasons. Remember? Your B-list self punched A-list Zach Monroe's face on set. You gave him—and your career—a nasty black eye." she shook her head as Ollie grunted angrily.

"Sounds to me like he's tired of being famous, Ms. Von Feldt. My arm's getting a bit tired, I might accidentally let go." The sarcasm was thick in his words, as well as amusement. "We can drive the car off the edge Thelma and Louise style and pretend like it was all a terrible accident." Alan offered this suggestion with a totally serious expression that made her wonder for a moment how well she actually knew him.

Ollie released a string of colorful curses and threats, continuing to writhe and shake. It was almost like he wanted to fall.

"Sounds like a good plot for an action movie." Stephanie prodded. "Such a shame the leading man here won't be in the business much longer. I bet that's a role he'd love to play." She pretended to think about it for a moment and gave a sigh. "No, that's no good. I was very publicly seen with him and I'm not interested in a murder trial."

Alan's left eyebrow raised, and at her slight nod, his fingers around Ollie's ankle loosened a bit.

"Ms. Von Feldt, this joker knew he was bringing you to an isolated area and that he wasn't supposed to leave the city." Alan casually switched which hand he was holding Ollie by, that eyebrow still raised at Stephanie. "He put his hands on you without your permission. You're most likely not the first date he's tried that with. He called you a bitch. Since you don't want me to let him go to see if he bounces well on rock, should we at least release the audio from your attempted sexual assault to the press?" The square planes of Alan's face were taut with displeasure, his dark eyes menacing.

Ollie started to make a series of strangled noises and then tumbled directly into a really pitiable display of begging.

"You can't! Please, I promise, it was just a mistake! I'll be better! I'll do better! Please!"

Stephanie walked a bit closer, her own fear of heights keeping her well back from the actual edge, despite the knee-high metal railing. Her eyes met Ollie's, and he must have been afraid of what he saw in the amber depths, because the less than eloquent, although *deeply* heart-felt apology began to bubble out of him, along with some actual tears. It was really kind of a shame to see him in such a state.

"I'm sorry! I'm sorry! I swear, I won't ever do it again!" No small man himself, the model and up-and-coming action star was getting alarmingly red in the face. Alan didn't seem to be breaking a sweat, and somehow still dwarfed the action star by what felt like a whole other person.

Like David Bautista standing next to Chris Pratt. Both were large, fit men, but one could clearly out-muscle the other.

Not a single car had passed by since Ollie parked in the turnoff and attempted to take advantage of perks their arranged date definitely wasn't offering. The fact that he broke contract, left the restaurant and then Los Angeles proper to bring her to a very specific and totally isolated spot at a canyon overlook had given her all the creepy feels.

The second she had realized what was happening, Stephanie turned in the cushy leather seat of his pretentious Tesla and pressed the panic button on her phone, alerting her agent and bodyguard both of her location. Thankfully the app was equipped to send out an emergency call to the office, activate her GPS location and start recording. She would need to thank Maxwell again for his connections and genius in developing and getting all that set up.

It hadn't been more than a few minutes alone with Ollie in the car and Alan had yanked her client out by the collar of his shirt. The look on Ollie's face had been quite the picture. Had Stephanie not been wrapped up in fending off his advances and attempting to open the door to escape, she might have gotten one. Ollie Parkinson was not her first client, but it seemed he would be the first utter contract failure. The idea made Stephanie stiffen—she didn't like not finishing a project and absolutely detested failing—but this was on him, not her.

"We can't all be brawn *and* beauty, I suppose." Stephanie said, motioning for Alan to let Ollie go—on the safe side of the guardrail.

Alan beamed at her compliment but seemed a bit sad that the model slash actor couldn't be dangled a bit longer. Or dropped further than a few inches.

Sandy hair now less than artfully disheveled, blue eyes bright with fear and rage, Ollie got to his feet, the blood slowly draining away from his tomato-colored (but still obnoxiously handsome) face. There would be a bit of a shiner on his right side for sure, and his lip was still swelling where she'd split it with her fist.

He scrambled toward Stephanie as though he'd be safer nearer the woman he'd tried to assault in the car. The woman with plenty of self-defense training who had not been afraid to use her stiletto heel as a weapon. The sight of the small, round bruises on his forehead and neck brought her some satisfaction.

"Look, I misunderstood. I'm sorry. *So* sorry. I'll never touch you again, I swear."

"You are absolutely right. You definitely won't."

Stephanie angled her body toward Ollie who was holding his hands up in an 'I surrender' gesture. His aqua gaze flicked nervously from the mountainous Alan, a retired MMA fighter, back to Stephanie.

"I can appreciate that you may have misunderstood the guidelines of our relationship Ollie, even though it's plainly written out in the contracts you signed. So, let's be extra clear—I am an actress, not a prostitute. You do not go off script, not even for a moment when you are with me—which is clearly outlined. We go to designated locations and perform our parts as clearly dictated in the paperwork. There is no touching, no kissing, no interaction that is not plainly stated in writing. This was a pretend relationship. One meant to bolster your career and nothing more."

Ollie appeared to have decided that he wanted to be famous after all. His nods were very enthusiastic. Too bad for him it was far too late.

"I swear, I get it. Totally understand now, only what's in the paperwork. I'm really very sorry. Just a big misunderstanding." His impeccably manicured hand rubbed idly at the spots on his forehead and neck where he got nailed with her heel.

"I'm sorry, Ollie, you seem to be misunderstanding. I'm not re-educating you for how this might go forward. The contract is null and void because of your bad decisions."

He visibly tensed, fists clenching. Alan adjusted his stance just a fraction, and Ollie backed down, looking oddly resigned.

"Shit. My agent is going to *kill* me."

"Probably. She still gets paid in full even though you screwed up." Alan's smirk was wide as he angled a thumb Stephanie's direction.

Ollie was very plainly horrified at this revelation.

"He's right. You blew it, Mr. Parkinson." Stephanie began to tap on her phone. "I'm also reporting you to my agent and attorney, who will spread the word far and wide about how you choose to treat your dates. Any retaliation and the audio goes out. Understood?"

He looked murderous but gave a tight nod.

"Go home, Ollie. My agent will be in touch with your team. We're done here."

Ollie's eyes flashed in anger, but it now seemed more toward himself than her. Clearly stunned by having screwed up that spectacularly again, he turned toward his vehicle, slamming the door once he slumped inside.

Revving the engine of a Tesla just didn't have the desired effect Stephanie was sure he was after, but he did it with gusto anyway. His very manly tantrum by car made her smile despite her frustration with the whole situation.

Her eyes tracked the Tesla as far as they could down the darkening stretch of road, her shoulders relaxing and dropping away from her ears a bit once he vanished from sight.

ONCE SAFELY IN Alan's gigantic SUV, Stephanie finally let out a shaky breath, stomach rolling and head pounding as her adrenaline crashed. She could feel him looking her over carefully as she fastened her seatbelt.

"You really alright, my girl?" A long-time friend of her father's, Alan had always been a safe, familiar face despite his imposing size and formidable strength. To her, he was like an uncle and overgrown teddy bear; even when he was dangling her terrible dates off the side of cliffs. Hell, that might have earned him extra hugs, to be honest.

Her head bobbed gently as she appraised her body.

"Yeah. I'm okay. That was intense." She forced a large breath out of her body and then another in. "He got a little handsy, but I took care of myself okay."

Alan let loose a proud, toothy grin. "Yeah, you did. That little asshole is going to have stiletto-print tattoos on his smug face for weeks."

A small laugh burst out of her as Alan's eyes tracked Ollie's Tesla pulling away from the overlook. After a beat, he began to follow him down the quiet highway toward Los Angeles.

"I hate loose ends." She sighed, fingers speedily moving over her phone screen, emailing her agent and lawyer about what happened so they could draw up her exit paperwork and spread the word to everyone they knew about Ollie. He'd be extremely lucky to not be blacklisted completely.

Alan shrugged. "If they don't act right, you cut them loose. No need for that mess in your life—that's why Samuel and Marty wrote that fine print saying you get full payment if they screw it up. You did your part, Steph. This is his fault."

"He was a perfect gentleman the whole time we were at dinner. Manners and by-the-book smiles. The whole works." A disappointed sigh escaped her lips.

A growl filled the cabin of the massive SUV. "Maybe he's not as terrible an actor as he's billed then. There's no way this was the first time he brought a girl up there to have his way."

Nodding, Stephanie closed her eyes for a moment and breathed deep. "Where were you that you got up there so fast?"

Glancing over, she saw a mischievous smirk on Alan's face. "You weren't the only one with a date tonight, my girl."

Stephanie smiled. "Who's the lucky lady? Anyone I know?"

Alan shook his head roughly. "Nope. Not going there with you. Your dad likes to gossip too much."

Stephanie laughed and it made her feel 100 pounds lighter. It could have been really, really bad if Alan hadn't been on call and close. Feeling safe in his car joking about his secret date was a most pleasant turn of events.

"That's rude. *I* can keep secrets just fine." Alan raised an eyebrow at her. Stephanie shook her head again. "Alright old man. Keep your secrets. Dad will find out eventually and tell me anyway."

"I have no doubt about that," Alan grumbled. "You and me? We're apples and caramel when you have a client." He pointed a finger and her then his thumb at himself. "Doesn't matter who I'm dating—*you're* my girl as long as you're in business with any twat needing your help to make himself look better."

There was really no arguing with that. Not that she really wanted to.

DURING THE EXIT interview later that week, Marty reported back that Ollie's team had sincerely hoped he'd get invited to her parents' Thanksgiving Party as the end-game to bolstering his status. That party, billed around town as *the* holiday event to attend, would have proved that he'd made it to the A-list.

Stephanie didn't feel bad at all that he'd been fired as her client and would never make it to the party. He was a mediocre actor, passable model and by all appearances, an awful human being. She'd been used by much better men than Ollie Parkinson to get to the party over the years.

She celebrated the beginning and end of her time with him by opening a bottle of champagne, ordering take-out from Mr. Woo and promising herself a long rest period before considering a new client, and perhaps expanding her selection criteria so she never had to deal with that mess ever again.

CHAPTER

Two

STEPHANIE PACED ACROSS the lush navy carpet of the sun-dappled home office as she spoke to her agent on the phone.

"I'm the one who told you I was ready for another job, Marty. Call them back. Set it up. I promise I'm ready."

Marty sighed audibly on the other end of the connection.

Her Godfather and agent since she was a child, he seemed unsure about continuing her business dealings since the Ollie Parkinson debacle, despite the fact that they had been quite successful before he had become their first canceled contract—and it had garnered them both quite a bit of money.

"Alright kid. Look, this is likely to go through really fast. I'll get in touch with Samuel and have him draw up the documents."

Samuel was another long-time family friend as well as her attorney. He was also her best friend Maxwell's father.

"Sounds good, Marty. Thank you for watching out for me. I appreciate it. Really, I do. But I'm the C.I.A.—I got this, right? It's in my blood. You don't have to worry so much about me." Her lips ticked up in a grin. She knew he'd see through the false bravado, but said the words anyway.

The sigh he gave this time was followed by a gritty chuckle.

"Sure kid. Celebrity Image Adjuster extraordinaire. I know you got a good head on your shoulders and your parents raised you right. But still, I love you like my own daughter and worry about you whether you want me to or not. Take care of yourself, okay?"

"You got it, Marty." Stephanie allowed herself a smile as she disconnected from the call. She could picture the salt-and-pepper haired man on the other end of the phone, hunched over his massive mahogany desk in a dress shirt that had cost more than most fancy shoes and a silk tie that was never quite straight. His glasses would likewise be slightly askew but his focus intent on the paperwork and phone in front of him.

Stephanie smiled.

Marty Dennison had always been part of her life and never stopped taking care of her. She loved him, and all of his quirky overbearing tendencies. He and Samuel had always been a great foil to her parents' much more carefree

approach to child-rearing. She and Maxwell had both ben-
efitted from 'uncle' Marty's love and antics.

Which reminded her—she was long overdue a phone
call to Maxwell. Growing up as they had, it had been nice
to have someone to share the experience with. Maxwell
could complain about Samuel's (comparatively) iron fist
and Stephanie could vent about the latest development in
hands-off, free-range parenting. They had been very good
friends for most of their lives, and even if their contact
lapsed for months at a time, they could always pick up
right where they left off.

Her amber gaze took in the lavish back yard through
the picture windows that formed the outside wall of the
office. There were birds playing in a broad stone birdbath,
bushes and plants and vines in full flower. The grandiose
Italian-tiled swimming pool shimmered teal and pearl
and called out in welcome to her, promising that summer
was nearly there.

With a deep breath, Stephanie placed the antiquated
cordless phone receiver that her mother simply wouldn't
retire back on the charging cradle and took a seat at the
double-sided cherry desk. Hers was the one facing the
outside, her mother's the one facing the room. Marlowe
always joked that if she sat looking out the windows, she
would never get anything accomplished. If she was being
honest about it, Stephanie often found herself daydreaming
instead of working because of the view.

The computer gave a quiet whir as she brought it back to life by moving the mouse around and she quickly tapped out business-related emails to both Marty and Samuel to begin the paper trail for this contract. After a moment's thought, she fired off a third message, a personal note to her parents who were traveling in Europe.

All that tidied up, she spun the chair around, leaned back into the supple leather and stretched. Her eyes traveled over the floor to ceiling bookshelves, the high priced and high-end interior designer placed accessory items like a jar full of seashells, blown glass vases and paperweights and shadowboxes of feathers and leaves. Scattered throughout were some of her mother Marlowe's many awards. By the books with antique leather bindings a SAG award, over near the window on a tiny glass shelf a Golden Globe. On the mantle of the purely decorative fireplace, surrounded by family photos, one of her two Oscars. The other was in the main guest bath down the hall—everyone loved to pose in the mirror with Oscar.

Stephanie frowned.

There was nothing of hers in this room. It felt cold without her mother's enormous, glowing presence there to share it. Her mother, an actress and long-time icon of Hollywood couldn't help but warm and fill a space with effervescent life. While Stephanie by no means begrudged her parents the travel, they seemed to be doing non-stop the last few years, she did miss them.

Determined to enjoy her day, Stephanie got up, strode purposefully through the house, quickly changed into her new red and white polka dot bathing suit and went out to the shimmering pool, basking in the golden rays of the California sun and enjoying her last bit of peace for a while.

After tying her unruly chocolate brown hair into a knot on the top of her head, Stephanie rolled onto her stomach on the lounge chair. All around her birds chirped, a gentle breeze rustled the well-established trees and the beautiful myriad of flowers scented the air. There were lots of things to love about her parents' Hollywood Hills home, but she had lately become strangely detached from it. After moving into her own space in another city, her parents' estate had begun to fall under the title of 'childhood home' in her mind. Stephanie was house-sitting while they were away, but longed to get back to her own loft.

The distance she felt from things that were so familiar was disconcerting and made her a little sad.

As she read a paperback romance and soaked in vitamin D, Stephanie's mind wandered. She couldn't help but go into work mode. Signing a new contract meant public appearances, paparazzi and always keeping on her game face. She felt bone-deep exhaustion just thinking about it, but surely this one wouldn't be as bad as some had been.

There were only a couple that gave her the shivers just thinking about. Naturally, Ollie Parkinson came to mind.

For nearly four years Stephanie had been in business for herself as an actress. It was a complicated set of dealings, and she turned down 90% of her propositions. What she had made through four years and just more than a handful of clients had been enough for her to pad a decent bank account wholly separate from her childhood actress earnings and the money her parents set aside for her in trust.

Marty was protective because her business could be dangerous—she was no fool, she knew exactly why he so carefully watched out for her. Samuel, Maxwell, and Alan were never far behind, not to mention her own father.

The contracts had to be very explicit and had taken months of re-working to get nearly perfect. The intake questionnaires were similarly exhaustive but no different than a serious online dating or matchmaking profile. Knowing your partner's favorite color, best friend's name and broad likes and dislikes could be significant to selling a relationship as genuine.

Stephanie was the C.I.A.—Celebrity Image Adjuster. She was in the business of contracting out her acting services to other actors or celebrities who needed a famous, clean reputed girlfriend to bolster their standing in Hollywood. Coming from the pedigree that she did, with Marlowe Von Feldt—the legendary actress—as a mother and Peter Von Feldt—a much sought-after composer for films—as a father, Stephanie certainly fit that bill. She had never been in trouble with the law, never been spotted doing anything illicit and maintained a very old-Hollywood good-girl image. Her acting career on film was limited to some work as a child and young adult, but behind the scenes, her business as the C.I.A. was thriving. It was all very hush-hush, but if you had a need and an in, there were a handful of others like her around. Nobody knew the particulars of course, but it was well known that such things happened.

In truth, real or fake, the publicity was good for everyone involved, and as long as all parties understood that it was just an act but the press never caught on, it was a good gig.

It was also safe.

Real relationships were not something Stephanie had any good experiences with, and having a secret job where performing a scripted relationship as an actress for payment kept her from having to actually meet anyone or put herself out there.

Safe.

Lonely.

Same thing, maybe. But protection for her heart took priority.

Realizing she had been staring at the same word for at least ten minutes while her mind had wandered, Stephanie tossed the book aside and plunged into the deep end of the pool with a graceful dive. The water was crisp and cooler than she would have liked, but it was only early April; not warm enough for the Summer sun to warm it quite yet and her parents didn't leave the heater running most of

the time since there was just no need except in the coldest
winter months.

She began swimming in long strokes from one end of
the Italian tiled pool to the other, killing her mind's worries
with exertion. Lap after lap, smooth glide and breath in to
breath out, slowly the details slipped from her thoughts.
Only when she could no longer feel her arms and her legs
were dragging low as though there were weights attached
did she emerge from the water.

To Stephanie's surprise, the sun was sitting low in
the sky. A glance at her phone as she toweled off showed
she had been in the water for nearly two hours. Stomach
grumbling, she gathered her things and she headed toward
the house.

AFTER A QUICK shower and dressing in a comfortable
t-shirt and yoga pants—something she would never consider wearing either outside the house or in the presence
of her 'image is everything, even in one's own home'
mother—Stephanie threw together a salad and sandwich
for dinner and instead of relaxing with her meal in front
of the television or while curled up with a good book, she
made the mistake of taking it with her into the office and
checking her email and the fax once more.

The paperwork was all waiting for her, one copy elec-
tronically, one via fax sitting in her printer tray in true

old-school Marty style. For real though, who even had fax anymore? The notion made her lips tick up once again. She really did love the man.

Stephanie flipped through the stack of pages with one hand and ate her sandwich with the other, scanning for any discrepancies, making notes where she wanted changes and finally signing off. No doubt Marty and Samuel would both make the changes and send the whole set back to her for final signatures within 24 hours, no matter that it was the weekend.

"Really?" Stephanie mused aloud to the empty room as she noted who the client was supposed to be. "Devon Greene? Why in the world does he need any help with good press?"

Frowning, most of her dinner forgotten at her elbow on the desktop, Stephanie began doing searches on Devon Greene on the computer. Tabloid sites, search engines, movie databases—the tabs fanned out across her taskbar.

Everything she found showed what she already knew, that he was currently playing a vampire on a wildly successful TV show about paranormal creatures coming out in a small town and all the young adult angst that such a situation might entail. Some of his acting history was unknown to her, but overall, he had been very successful since his teen years and hadn't ever been in trouble for booze or drugs or any of the normal things that led actors to her for image help. He even ran an animal sanctuary and rescue foundation with his brothers and dabbled in other charity work.

By all appearances, he was pretty perfect. Arrogant maybe, but that was pretty much a requirement for any leading man.

Stephanie had watched the show, and some of his other shows in the past. He was pretty dreamy as far as such things went, with that ridiculously angular jawline, slim nose and icy blue eyes. His current show had his hair dyed jet black, and the contrast with his eyes was just that much more striking. He certainly fit the bill of handsome young actor.

Unable to stop working once she started, her fingers dialed Marty's office number.

He answered the phone with a dry chuckle. "It's after five on a Friday night, kid, shouldn't you be out doing something fun?"

"I could ask you the same, old man. What are you still doing at the office? Why aren't you out to dinner with Penelope? That's the least you could do for her staying married to you all these years."

Marty guffawed with laughter. "My girl, you have no idea. God's honest truth you speak. I married a damn saint." He paused and sighed. "But I know you didn't call to remind me to buy my wife a nice dinner and maybe flowers or something sparkly, though I probably should thank you for doing so. What's up?"

"What's the deal with Greene? He doesn't need my help."

"That's my girl!" Marty laughed again. "See? Now, it's days like today I remember how unlike some of your contemporaries you are. I thought you might ask." Marty cleared his throat, and Stephanie could hear him take a drink from his Friday evening bourbon. Ice clinking in a glass reached her through the phone line. It was so familiar; she could see him doing it in her mind from the million times she had seen him do it in his office or in her father's den. It made her smile. "He was talking to his PR team, and they recommended he find a girl, you know, to fire up the female fan-base."

"Unattainable is always more desirable." Stephanie could feel the cynical smile forming on her lips, but couldn't stop it. There had been a number of reasons she had moved to another city and worked hard and being on the fringes of the business unless it suited her needs.

"You got it, kiddo. Still time to say no. We only got your prelim sign off, and Samuel hasn't done up the new version with your changes in the legal just yet."

Stephanie sighed and leaned back in the leather chair, eyes focusing on the giant stone birdbath which was now illuminated by upturned garden lights in the blue twilight.

"No," She said, but her tone still felt as though it had a question mark in it. More firmly, she added, "No. It's a good change of pace I guess." Stephanie pinched the bridge of her nose. "At least it's not more drug recovery publicity or trying to back-pedal your image after being slapped with assault charges, right?"

Marty laughed, a full-on guffaw. "I love you kid. You've got a unique perspective on things." The sound of ice in an empty glass traveled to her again. "Let me call Samuel. I'll get you the revised contract before the weekend is out. I suspect this guy wants to get started next week as hard as his team is pushing us to get the paperwork done."

"Sounds good, Marty. Have a good weekend, okay?"

"You too, kid. I'm sure Penny will want to express her thanks in advance for her fancy dinner and new jewelry."

"She's most welcome. You know where to find me, Marty."

Stephanie hung the cordless up again, resumed her searches and frowned at the screen.

"What exactly are you after, Devon Greene?"

CHAPTER
Three

TRUE TO HIS word, Marty had the revised contract waiting for her in the office Sunday morning. Stephanie scanned it, then read it thoroughly just in case, signed off and sent it back before diving into the completed dating profile questionnaire.

"Alright. Let's do this." Stephanie muttered to herself as she tapped the send button on the electronic version, then punched in Marty's home fax number on the printer.

She spent her Sunday sorting out work-appropriate clothing in the walk-in closet of her childhood bedroom. Designer dresses went to the left side of her bed, blouses and slacks went right. Designer jeans and t-shirts and other casual wear went to the center. Carefully matching shoes and handbags and jewelry to complete the outfits was next, and there was a satisfying sense of accomplishment to finding perfect matches.

All these efforts were basically Stephanie channeling her mother, but it was necessary.

Given a choice, she would never go to such lengths, would be perfectly happy to lounge around in gauzy sun-dresses and sandals or yoga pants and t-shirts. This was a never-ending source of shock and despair to the always well-put-together and ethereally beautiful Marlowe.

"Where did my little girl go? The one who loved pink frilly dresses and glittery high heels and princess hair-dos?" Her mother had lamented one day when Stephanie had been a teenager and couldn't be convinced to dress in anything other than torn blue jeans and concert t-shirts.

"Moooom." Stephanie had stretched the word to at least eight syllables. "I'm not six anymore!"

Stephanie had been in an angsty teenager phase, but never forgot the wounded look on her mother's beautiful face; the particular way she pressed her lips into a line when she had hurt feelings but wouldn't say anything to lash out at others to make them feel as badly as she did.

To make up for her grunge phase and being a normal, hormonal, and just plain rude teenager to her mother, Stephanie had allowed Marlowe to take her shopping and teach her the ins and outs of high fashion. It made no sense to Stephanie, and it was not something she cared about keeping up with, but she did it for her mom. When Stephanie managed to put together an outfit and accessories properly, Marlowe always glowed with happiness and her graceful hands would rise palm-to-palm up by her face, a broad smile lighting up her expressive almond-shaped eyes.

People had always told Stephanie that she had her mother's eyes, but she didn't. Marlowe's were a beautiful buttery toffee color, whereas Stephanie's were a warm brandy. Stephanie didn't dislike her unique color, but her mother's hue always seemed just that much more striking and lovely to her.

Her cell phone rang just as Stephanie was getting ready to watch a movie. She set aside the bowl of popcorn and sighed. The number was listed only as Client. That could only mean that Marty was having the call routed through from the agency switchboard.

This was one of the many security features of their arrangement, and it came in very handy for Stephanie to not have to travel with multiple phones. She could keep her private number private and still accept Client calls without the risk of her personal phone number being shared around the city. Clients called a designated number that rang through to the agency, and the calls were routed through to her cell from there. It was genius—Maxwell had come up with it.

She resolved to call him once again. She missed talking to him.

Stephanie hesitated, finger hovering above the accept icon. The negotiation phase and paperwork for Devon Greene weren't quite finished. She didn't have any other active clients, but she wasn't technically on the clock quite yet. With a sorrowful glance at her popcorn, and against better judgment, Stephanie answered it before voice-mail could pick up.

"Hello?"

"Hi." There was a thoughtful pause. "Um, I'm sorry, I wasn't expecting anyone to answer, actually."

"Who's calling please?" Stephanie could feel the frown on her face and forced herself to relax those muscles.

"Ah, this is Devon? Devon Greene?" The rich tenor was tense.

"You don't sound so sure." Stephanie teased, instantly regretting the snarky edge to her tone. It was her own irrational nervousness that always came with a new client that she was upset about. To her great surprise, he laughed.

"I'm sure. Sorry, I'm … honestly, I am a little nervous."

"No," She pushed out a long breath. "I'm sorry. Usually, direct phone calls don't really start until we're through all the final paperwork. I'm just a little surprised is all." Stephanie started a slow pace around the living room.

"If I'm interrupting anything, I can call back another time." He sounded remorseful. That made Stephanie feel extra bitchy.

"No, it's fine, really. What can I do for you, Mr. Greene?" Stephanie reigned in her bad attitude and pushed herself into polite business mode.

"Devon, please. Mr. Greene sounds … well, anyway, I was going over the contracts? And I had a few questions.

I thought it would be best if I called to discuss them with you directly."

"That's fine, but we generally advise changes or concerns be discussed with the intermediaries just for security purposes. If anything is being changed, we'll have to have new documents drawn up anyhow so that saves a step." She paused, hating how clinical she sounded and noting his heavy silence on the other end of the line. "We can talk about what has you worried and if it requires getting others involved, I'll just stop you, okay?"

The sigh he heaved was audible. Whatever had him wound up must be serious, Stephanie mused. He really was that nervous. The notion actually settled her a bit. At least they were in this awkward first phone call thing together.

"Yes. That sounds perfect." He took a deep breath. "Okay, so there's a section here about dating procedures? And there's a bunch of legalese I don't really understand. Can you just…break that down for me?"

Stephanie actually laughed. His honesty was refreshing.

"Sure. Quite simply, we go on dates. I prefer it if we can have at least 48 hours' notice to plan. This is basically a scripted performance of a relationship. I want to be very clear about that. You are paying me to be an actress, not an escort."

His tone got very serious. "Absolutely, I understood that right off."

Stephanie sighed lightly and felt her shoulders drop a bit. Good, at least there was no confusion there. "Once we have a chance to meet in person we will finalize hard limits around physical contact, date duration, relationship length, all the fine points. The basics are lined out in the contracts you have now, but I like to do a much more detailed write up as an addendum once we have a chance to sit down and speak with one another in person. For a good starting point to get a feel for how this works, I would suggest your PR people let the press know we will be going to be at Chateau Marmont on Tuesday around 1 pm for a casual 'get to know you better' lunch. I can explain in detail and demonstrate the acting skills you will be paying me for."

"That sounds great," Devon chuckled. "Pick you up at 12:30?"

"Are you sending a car or driving yourself?"

"I hate using a driver unless I have to. Seems pretentious."

Stephanie cocked an eyebrow, the corner of her mouth lifting as well. She was beginning to get the feeling she might be quite glad she had agreed to this contract.

"I agree completely. I look forward to working with you, Mr. Greene."

"Devon." He corrected. "Thank you, Stephanie."

Stephanie agreed to have Marty forward her parents' address to Devon's people through the switchboard at the agency once Devon was off the line. Feeling much more relaxed about her upcoming assignment, she settled into a plush cashmere blanket and turned on her movie, glad to dive into a fictional world someone else had to think up before getting started with her new fake boyfriend.

CHAPTER *Four*

AT PRECISELY 12:30 a silver VW Eos pulled into the driveway. From the bank of video monitors in the alcove off the kitchen, Stephanie could see it was Devon Greene.

The same image would have appeared on her phone screen, but she had disabled that app—it tended to go off all hours of the night to tell her that a tree was moving in the wind or a bunny was nibbling on the succulents in the yard. She needed to ask Maxwell if there was a way to adjust the settings.

She buzzed him through the wrought iron gate at the street and prepared to meet him at the front door.

For the hundredth time, she smoothed the front of her Caroline Hererra dress. It was a lightweight Springtime dress with a V neck and no sleeves. The layers of silk were frothy around her thighs and ended just at her knees. The gentle pastel floral pattern made it feel very feminine. Stephanie's mother had bought it for her a couple of years back as a compromise of their styles. Paired with some pink strappy heeled sandals and a matching lavender cardigan, Stephanie thought her mother would be pleased.

One glance in the mirror in the entryway told her that her makeup was still un-smudged, hair pulled up into a severe ponytail maintaining its sleek look. The C.I.A. was operable. This was Stephanie on-stage. She realized she felt similarly about this persona that she created to work in as she did about her shared office with her mother. Stephanie was there … but not there. There was very little Real Stephanie in Image Adjuster Stephanie.

Stephanie exhaled, smoothed the dress just at her ribs one last time and opened the door after the bell chimed cheerily through the house.

Stephanie found herself looking at the top of Devon's head.

"Hi, I'm Devon Greene? Here to see Steph—" Devon finally looked up from the bouquet of lilies and daisies in his hands. "Oh." He smiled, a dazzling white grin that was no doubt part of the reason he was such a popular actor with young women. He seemed pleasantly surprised at her appearance and gave her a quick up and down sweep of his eyes. "Hi. I didn't expect you to answer the door yourself."

Stephanie smiled. She could feel that it didn't quite reach her eyes. It was her stage smile; one she had worked very hard to perfect.

"Nice to meet you, Mr. Greene." He cocked his head to the side looking a bit uncomfortable, and she corrected herself, the smile turning genuine. "Sorry. Nice to meet you, Devon."

"The pleasure is mine, I'm sure. I, ah, got these for you." He offered the flowers with a practiced flourish. "I didn't think my mother would appreciate me forgetting my first date manners whether it's a real date or not." He gave her a sly grin and a wink. Stephanie couldn't help warm a bit from his quick to smile, lighthearted attitude.

"They're beautiful, thanks." She gestured to the foyer. "Would you like to come in for just a moment? I can put these in some water and there are a few documents we need to look over and sign before we go."

"Sure." He flashed that million-dollar smile again, his icy blue eyes flashing. "You look quite lovely."

"Thank you. I like your shirt." Stephanie gestured vaguely to the light blue linen shirt he was wearing with black chinos. It matched the particular shade of his eyes exactly. She would have bet a large sum of money that he knew that, too. Or perhaps his stylist did.

Stephanie let him in and led him down the hall toward the kitchen so that she could find a vase and go over the basic paperwork before they left.

"So, this is the place where the legendary Thanksgiving parties happen." Devon's eyes wandered as he took in the long hall, well-polished travertine flooring and family photos on the walls. Interspersed with the photos were small paintings, some of them Stephanie's, and more of her parents' awards. Stephanie had always thought of the grand hallway as a kind of gallery, where all kinds of valuables were on display and ready for itchy fingers to make off with.

"This is the place. What have you heard about Thanksgiving?" Stephanie felt her senses tingle a bit. Marty knew that Devon was picking her up, and she wasn't overly worried about her safety, but having any strangers in her parents' home suddenly seemed like a not very well thought out plan.

The fact that he was mentioning Thanksgiving right off the bat had her defenses up. Getting invited to that party had been the sole goal of a handful of would-be suitors and former friends over the years.

"You can't work anywhere in this town without knowing of the Von Feldt Thanksgiving parties. If you believe the rumors all around town about it, if you get invited you know you've finally made it." He paused at a particularly flattering family photo. Stephanie had been sixteen when it was taken. Next to it was a six-inch square canvas she had painted as a tiny landscape of her view out the office window. She watched as he leaned in and squinted and the painting, then smiled broadly. "They don't make houses like this anymore. It's really something else. Gorgeous, even." He finally turned his gaze back to her.

"I'll tell my parents you think so." Stephanie smiled politely, leading him into the very recently remodeled French style kitchen.

She pulled a vase down from one of the cabinets, filled it with water from the graceful chrome swan-neck faucet and fluffed the blooms as she settled them down into the vessel. "There. Lovely." They really were. Stephanie gave Devon a genuinely appreciative smile. "So. The contracts. This is more of the same of what you've signed off on in negotiations…" Stephanie felt herself drop fully into business face, explaining the clearly defined language around transportation, physical contact and what was expected in general for conduct.

"Okay, so straight there and back, no detours or dangerous behavior on the roads." He looked serious and nodded as he recited it back to her.

"Right. Physical contact shall be limited to prompted and or scripted hand-holding, approved touch on arm or back to demonstrate that we are familiar with one another, that kind of thing. Clear?" Stephanie raised her eyes to his with a brusque glance and he nodded, initialing on the paper next to the words. "Great. Give me just a moment to send these to the agency. Then, shall we go?" She collected the papers neatly, tapping them straight on the granite.

Eyes flashing, a lopsided grin on his face, he nodded and waited in the hallway for her while she quickly scanned the forms to Marty, and then he allowed her to lead them out of the house. Once at the car, his manners took over once again and he opened her door.

"Thank you." Stephanie slid carefully into the sporty sedan.

As Devon navigated them across town to the restaurant, Stephanie took charge of the conversation to fill in her dossier for him. She had enough practice at these kinds of conversations that it seemed friendly, but really, she was taking mental notes to help improve the ruse they were putting on.

"So, Devon. Why is it that you've decided to hire a girlfriend?"

He glanced at her and began to laugh. Stephanie was gathering that his laid-back attitude was no come on, it was genuine. He seemed quick to laugh and easy to get along with.

She picked at a loose thread on her skirt.

"Direct. I like it." Devon nodded his approval and looked at her as they sat at a stoplight. "Well, real girlfriends haven't always been my strong suit." He explained with an awkward shrug. Traffic began to move so he turned his gaze from her and put it back on the road. "I thought this might be a slightly less messy way to accomplish the goal."

"The goal being…?"

"My team thinks I'm more desirable to the 18–35 female demographic if I'm dating someone." He made a face, his tone indicating he was repeating exactly what they had said to him in regard to the subject. "While that may be true, I'm not sure why it's up to me to increase the show's ratings. There's a bunch of us on the cast. Maybe the writers could listen to the fans and give them more of what they want…" He heaved a sigh and shook his head. "Sorry. I feel like this is all a bit silly. No offense."

"None taken. I understand completely. Likely you're the biggest draw—I've seen it before." Stephanie cocked her head to one side, giving a slight shrug. She filed away his feelings about the situation, knowing it was valuable information for how their partnership would work. A thought occurred to her. "Unless it's not the female demographic you'd rather be attracting? Makes no real difference for how we play this, to be honest."

Devon sputtered a laugh. "No, I'm definitely interested in women. I just don't have much luck with dating."

Stephanie nodded, a strange sense of relief washing over her. "Well, in that case, try to feel special, not just singled out. It doesn't change anything, but it makes the situation slightly less ridiculous."

He glanced at her, noting her genuine expression. He chuckled again as he pulled up to the valet stand. "That's a great way to look at it, actually. And I apologize. This is your legitimate job, and I just insulted you."

Stephanie stared at him a moment, shocked. A warm tingle surged to her chest and warmed her cheeks. "No offense taken." Her lips raised upward, the flushed skin feeling a bit too tight on her face as she did so.

A young man helped Stephanie out of the car, and as soon as Devon took her elbow to guide her into the restaurant, dozens of voices asking questions that all sounded the same began on either side of them. Men and women with every kind of camera from smart-phone to traditional telephoto lens were snapping shots of them to sell off to the highest tabloid bidder. Devon's people had done a great job of spreading the word about their date.

Stephanie tensed and noticed Devon likewise stiffen. That old saying about the world being a stage? All too true. Stephanie's stage smile began to ache her face only moments in. Devon's expression somehow managed to put off a vibe of quiet acknowledgment of his coolness factor and subtle appreciation. Stephanie realized she would have to up her game in that regard as they strolled past the gaggle of paparazzi to the hostess stand inside. She suddenly felt out of practice. Image Adjuster Stephanie was rusty from lack of use.

Once seated out on the lavish terrace, the snick noise of pictures being taken resumed, but only intermittently and far into the background. There was a heavy flowering hedge serving as a fence, and the photographers were not allowed inside the restaurant. A few very clever ones were standing on dumpsters to get a few prime photos of any celebrities that might be having lunch. Since it was part of the deal that the paparazzi had been tipped off of their date, the pair gracefully pretended to ignore them.

After placing their order with a waitress that clearly recognized them but admirably kept herself from drooling over Devon or squealing even a little, Devon and Stephanie began what Stephanie liked to call the training wheels date.

Stephanie carefully crossed her ankles and propped her chin on her hand, eyes new-relationship adoring, body angled toward Devon. Voice low, she began to coach him on how they could maximize their first date for the press.

"I'm going to walk you through this." She said quietly, smile still firmly in place. "We're just starting to date, right? This is the get-to-know-you lunch. Whatever you say, I'm going to find funny, or fascinating or both, even if you're describing how exactly you floss those pearly whites every day."

Devon nodded, took a sip of his water and then likewise put on one of his casual but very endearing grins.

"You're the expert. I'm putty in your hands." He likewise leaned against the table with an elbow, his shocking blue eyes gazing at her with feigned adoration, a playful wiggle of his eyebrows nearly making her laugh.

Stephanie felt a tiny, foreign flash of heat in her stomach. The fleeting thought—If only that were true—zipped through her mind before she could stop it. Silently scolding herself, outwardly doing nothing more than gazing sweetly at her date, her business-self buckled down and pushed any kind of emotion out of her mind. She was actually a bit angry with herself for breaking character. For feeling anything at all, really.

Real feelings have no place in this kind of business. Stephanie had learned that a long, long time ago.

Their waitress delivered a small basket of bread and their drinks and was gone with a flip of her blonde ponytail. Stephanie noticed that the waitress's pants were about three sizes too small, making it impossible not to notice her adorably tiny heart-shaped rear-end. Stephanie waited for Devon's gaze to stop following the waitress. Once his eyes met hers, she gave a knowing smile. He grinned like a letch, both admitting and not caring that he'd been caught.

To be fair, it was a great ass.

"When lunch comes, we're going to eat, and laugh, and otherwise act as though we're perfectly into one another. Simple enough?" She punctuated her question with a broad smile.

"Sure. I can definitely handle that." He picked up a piece of the fresh sourdough bread and began to butter it. After taking a bite, a thought occurred to him. "You said you've seen this kind of situation before—like why they want me to be dating. How many times exactly?"

Putting a coy grin on her face that was only partly to please the press that might be watching, she leaned back in her chair and sipped at her sparkling water.

"Wouldn't you like to know?"

He laughed.

"Trade secret?"

"You bet. C.I.A. is a clever acronym for me and my business for lots of reasons." She winked at him. Flirty

Stephanie was never seen in the wild. She thanked her years of acting lessons for her level of skill in being able to pull off the face and body language that went with Flirty since her real-life practice was quite lacking in that area. The quiet click of pictures being taken sounded a few times, then was quiet again. She realized then how much her love/hate relationship with that noise and the reason for it had become quite unbalanced and heavy on the hate side.

Stephanie reveled in the comfort of the wicker seat, recalling the dozens of times her mother had brought her here for brunch, or a casual girls' lunch. The small grass lawn was impeccably mowed, the flowering bushes lending a lovely pink decoration and gesture of sweet fragrance. The April sunshine was warm and comforting on her shoulders despite the large umbrella above them and the cool gentle breeze that occasionally fluttered her skirt and ponytail.

Their waitress was back again fairly quickly, delivering Stephanie's salad and Devon's soup and sandwich. She managed to get in another coy smile in Devon's direction, but he shut her down by looking back at Stephanie after a quick thank you.

Stephanie's heart sped up and it took a moment for her to re-master it. What was wrong with her? The first rule in this business is to keep your feelings out. She took a deep breath to try and center herself.

Focusing on maintaining a look of total new relation-ship interest on her face and with her body, Stephanie guided Devon through some key body language.

"You'll see me cross and uncross my legs so I can lean closer—" She demonstrated, once again leaning toward him across the table as she daintily picked at her Salad Niçoise. "—because I'm just so interested in whatever you're saying." Stephanie went so far as to crinkle her eyes up at the corners with a bright smile and give a short laugh as though whatever she had said to him was highly amusing.

Devon, not pretending, laughed heartily. "This is like one long, acting exercise." He nodded, stirring his soup around with a spoon.

"Precisely." She speared a tomato with the tines of her fork and gently placed it in her mouth, chewing with a smile.

Devon winced and shifted in his seat. This made Stephanie unreasonably pleased with herself. Point one to Stephanie.

He placed one arm on the table, taking Stephanie's unoccupied hand into his on the linen tablecloth. Artificial shutter clicks sounded over their shoulders for what felt like a solid minute. Almost no conscious effort went into her coy smile and a quick dip of her head as though she were flustered to be touching him. She noted that his hands were warm and soft, and Stephanie wasn't entirely displeased that he was touching her. Both because it was an excellent move for the photogs and because it was a friendly but gentle grip. He ran his thumb over her knuckles, that famous adorable lopsided grin on his mouth, icicle blue eyes boring into her brandy ones.

"Well played, sir." She complimented. "Good use of the outlined physical contact." Her heart pounded behind her ribs, an electrical current thrilling her blood from his touch. Point one to Devon.

"That's why they pay me the big bucks."

After a moment, he let go of her hand and they finished their meal, practicing all the skills Stephanie had been describing. When they were finished, he paid the blonde waitress with cash and the pair left the terrace, Devon's hand gently placed between her shoulder-blades. Stephanie mentally noted that he had indeed been paying attention to the important pieces from the contract, and was pleased.

She was simultaneously furious with her traitor body for reacting so strongly to him and satisfied that this was going to be an excellent and outwardly natural-appearing business match. Their dating profiles had matched up very well.

Once safely back in the car, Stephanie let out a breath and appraised him with one eyebrow raised.

"Very well done, Mr. Greene."

"Devon, please—we're going to be a couple after all. And thank you. That was kind of fun." He gave a broad smile and navigated them back toward her parents' estate up Laurel Canyon Boulevard. "Even the torture part." He winked, and she felt the jolt of pleasure that incited all the way to her toes.

There was companionable silence as he drove her home. Once they had buzzed through the iron gate and pulled into the circular drive in front of the house, he turned to smile at her.

"I appreciate your help today, Stephanie. I had a nice lunch. I have a much clearer understanding of our agreement now."

"Glad to hear it. I enjoyed our meeting, Devon." More than she wanted to admit.

He got out of the car and came around to open her door. As he walked her to the house, she glanced at her phone, pulling up the calendar app.

"So, what's next?" He asked.

"Up to you. Dinner? Some kind of nature outing?" She stopped on the steps, fishing for her keys. "What would you normally do on a second date?"

He thought for a moment, fingers rubbing his chin.

"Dinner. Friday?"

"Sure." Stephanie made a quick note on her calendar as she opened the front door. "Anything else I can help you with at the moment?"

Devon shook his head.

Stephanie felt a rush of disappointment, then a flood of anger with herself. What was the matter with her?

"That's okay. I've got to be on set by 4. Night shoots all week." He gave a half-hearted grimace. "I'll call you to set up dinner."

"Sounds good." Her whole body began to tingle as he leaned in and kissed her cheek.

He looked shocked and a bit nervous as he pulled away.

"I'm sorry. I just…I felt like I needed to do that. I had a nice time. I didn't mean to overstep the approved contact. Especially after just getting an atta-boy for doing a good job." He chuckled, the sound the tiniest bit strained.

Stephanie smiled through a heady rush of hormones. "It's okay, no harm done. Thanks again for lunch."

Stephanie waited just inside the doorway until he was back in his car. He gave a raised arm wave and drove off.

Closing and locking the heavy over-sized wooden door, Stephanie immediately took down her hair and mussed it with her fingers, the roots sore from being pulled into such a tight ponytail. With a groan, she pushed her palms into her eyes. "Get it together Von Feldt. This will never do. Game face, remember?" She mumbled to herself. After a moment, she took a deep breath and pulled off the torturous shoes. She carried the heels to her room, slipped out of the dress and into her bathing suit.

Her mind was a mess. Her body was throwing out all kinds of inappropriate signals in regard to Devon Greene, and she couldn't have it. That doesn't work in a fake relationship.

It was not lost on her that her overwhelming need to get in the pool after their date was tantamount to taking a cold shower. Laps worked out her frustrations and eventually she was too exhausted to be mad at herself.

After a dinner of cold cereal, she sent a quick message to Marty about their intro date and told him she would get back on more of their scheduled dates once she had them blocked out. After a few quick notes to herself in Devon's official client dossier on her computer, she collapsed into bed, remembering just how tiring the fake smiles and bright expressions really were.

Never-mind actual real feelings. The exhaustion she felt from those and the hope … well that was nearly unbearable.

CHAPTER
Five

STEPHANIE'S PHONE WAS getting quite the workout.

She had just gotten off an hour-long conversation with her parents, who were now somewhere delightful in Spain when Devon called to plan dinner.

Headed toward the couch, she shuffled her phone and a bubble envelope with a photo-book her mother had assembled from their journey so far in her hands. After taking a seat, Stephanie had flipped through it and found herself smiling. Her parents were a beautiful couple and were very much enjoying their long vacation.

When the Client number flashed on her screen, Stephanie felt her pulse pick up. Her finger hesitated over the answer icon. After taking a deep breath, she connected the call. There wasn't even a moment's pause before he started speaking.

"Do you like sushi?"

"Normal people say hello first, Mr. Greene." Stephanie laughed, her own hello still lingering on her lips, feeling strange from not being said.

"Seems like a waste of time. So? Do you?"

"Do I what, say hello? Or think it's a waste of time?"

He chuckled. "Neither. Do you like sushi?"

"Sure, who doesn't?" Stephanie found herself grinning as she pulled a bottle of her mother's favorite flavored electrolyte water out of the fridge.

"You'd be surprised, I think. Nobu it is. Pick you up at seven?"

"I think I can pencil you in." Her tone was light and after hanging up with him still chuckling, she quickly set about gathering her things to make a trip to the salon and grocery store. Her celebrity was sometimes problematic when she wanted to do something simple, like go to the mall or get things at the grocery store, but she had learned how to just ignore and smile to get through her errands. She was recognizable, but mostly got left alone unless it was a slow press week or she happened to be working with a client and the goal was to be spotted out.

She guessed that it wasn't that interesting or lucrative to nab a photo of the good-girl Von Feldt daughter picking up her dry cleaning. That was perfectly fine with her. They did, however, always seem to catch her in the most unattractive pose when they did decide she was doing something worthy of capturing. Why did they do that? Nobody needed to see her double chin or her mouth hanging open and eyes half-closed.

Stephanie drove her father's black Land Rover to her stylist, who gave the ends a trim and added some new toffee-colored highlights to her chocolate hued hair. As the dye set, Stephanie flipped through a magazine.

"So…" Janice, the stylist asked, a smile on her lips. "Anything new with you?"

Stephanie looked up from the magazine and met the woman's playful gaze in the mirror. Janice lifted an eyebrow and peeked into one of the foils.

"I'm sure I don't know what you're talking about, Janice." Stephanie feigned ignorance, looking back at her magazine.

"Oh, you tease!" Janice teased, three other customers (all of different levels of celebrity themselves) and their stylists were now paying attention to her. It paid to have an exclusive hair salon in Beverly Hills.

Loudly, Janice declared, "Someone was spotted out to lunch with Devon Greene yesterday." Hands on her broad hips, deep brown eyes twinkling, Janice waited for Stephanie to respond.

There was a general chatter at this revelation, and Stephanie laughed, realizing that everyone was staring at her. One woman in particular, a tiny slip of a thing getting her nails done, was giving her a very interested stare. Stephanie felt like she might know the woman from somewhere, but couldn't quite place her. There was something about her blonde hair and the structure of her face that felt familiar.

"It was lunch, ladies. We didn't get hitched or anything important."

All at once over the titter fresh gossip in a salon always garners, Stephanie was fielding questions.

"Is he really that handsome in person?"

"What's he like?"

"Did you kiss?"

"What does he smell like?"

Stephanie laughed and shook her head, glancing down at her phone as it dinged, alerting her of a new text message.

"Seriously guys, just lunch. You all know he's gorgeous. Why don't you pull up TMZ and see what they have to say about my relationship? They usually know more than I do."

Janice muttered something like, "Ain't that the truth." and slightly disappointed, the rest of the salon went back to speculating on their own. The interested blonde woman smiled broadly and turned away from the conversation. Stephanie was puzzled by her. Did she work for a tabloid? She didn't seem malicious, just genuinely very curious.

Her phone pinged in her hand. The message flashed across the screen before she could put it face-down or in her purse.

D: *Have a minute to chat?*

Stephanie felt her shoulders tense as she saw it had come from Devon. There was no way Janice hadn't seen it. She was regretting having changed her phone's settings to display his name instead of Client.

"Oooh, now he's texting her." Janice was standing over Stephanie's shoulder.

Tiny interested blonde manicure woman spun around quickly and smiled at Stephanie again. She felt compelled to smile back, but she was beginning to get a little uncomfortable. The feeling that she should recognize the woman only intensified. Her mental catalog took extra note of her blonde hair and sharply defined, pixie-like features so she could think about it further.

Caught between being frustrated and glad for rumor-mill publicity sake that her message had been spotted, she could feel the flush in her cheeks as the whole room chattered about her message.

Shaking her head, she tapped out a response.

> **S:** *Not right at the moment. Maybe in an hour?*
> **D:** *Ok. Call you in an hour.*

Stephanie put her phone back in her purse as Janice pulled off the foils and rinsed out the dye.

Forty-five minutes later, her hair was cut, highlighted and styled within an inch of its life.

"You know I never do this much work to my hair at home, right?"

Janice placed a hand over her ample bosom, pretending to be wounded.

"Yeah, I know. I like to experiment with you because you never care what I do." Janice winked, took off the black cape and walked with Stephanie up to the register.

"Thank you, Janice. I'll be back in a few weeks."

"I know you will, honey. Those highlights are a bitch to maintain." Janice winked again, and without looking accepted the bills that Stephanie handed her.

With a wave, Stephanie said goodbye and ventured to her second stop.

She didn't need much, so the funky little grocery just a few doors down would suit her needs.

It was early afternoon on a Wednesday, so the crowd was relatively light, and there thankfully were no photographers hanging around.

Stephanie was examining labels on packages of trail mix when she felt a presence next to her.

"I like what you've done with your hair."

The tenor voice made Stephanie spin.

"Oh! Hi." She returned the friendly smile a very casual Devon was giving her. He had a day's worth of stubble on his chin and instead of making him look grungy, he looked rugged and if possible, even more handsome.

Her heart was once again charging along in her chest. Maybe she needed to see a doctor.

"Guess there's no need for that phone call now." He looked at the packages in her hands. "That one, no question." He pointed.

"Thanks." Stephanie put the rejected pouch down, placing the one he recommended in her basket. She was nervous and angry with herself for being so. She wasn't prepared for being approached unannounced out in the open. "What's up?"

"I had some questions. Do you need to finish shopping? We could go for coffee after if you like?" He paused, seeing the blank expression on her face. "Or … not? Do we need to make an appointment for coffee? Sorry, I'm not used to the rules yet, I guess."

"No, no. Coffee is fine." Stephanie tried to recover her carefully crafted composure, quickly gathered the remaining items on her short list as he followed her through the store, his own pile of items in a hand-basket.

They checked out, stashed their purchases in their respective cars and walked a few doors further down to a small coffee shop.

Lattes in hand, they sat on the patio.

"So, I've been running scenarios through my head, and I think I figured out how I think I want this to go," Devon said, pushing an empty sugar packet around the table with his finger. He glanced around the patio. Stephanie dug a small notebook and pen out of her purse. "Did you see the entertainment news last night?" He asked.

Stephanie shook her head. "No. I don't watch much TV."

His face pinched comically. "Isn't that against the natural order? Shouldn't you do it for like, professional research or something? Also, are you seriously taking notes with paper and pen? Do you not use your phone like the rest of us?"

Stephanie shrugged and laughed at his mock horror. "Probably. I'll try harder, I promise."

"See that you do." He teased. "Anyway. They were saying," Devon dropped his voice and leaned in conspiratorially, lopsided grin playful, eyes sparkling. "That we are the new trendy couple spotted out and about. I'm thinking we take that and run with it."

Stephanie smiled. It was only partly fake.

It was not even partly fake.

"What exactly did you have in mind?" She had to clear her throat to loosen the grip her pulse had on her breath.

"I'm thinking we do a burn hot and fizzle fast relationship. Two or three months maybe, we are out all the time, super into one another then BAM, can't stand each other. It's over."

Stephanie laughed in earnest, nearly choking on her coffee as he pantomimed the implied explosion.

"Alright. Noted. You have this all worked out?"

His eyes blazed with excitement.

"Yep. At least two dates a week, maybe three. Then we have our big blow out just in time for sweeps. The network will love all the press. Maybe I'll get a raise." Stephanie couldn't help but smile and laugh at his sense of humor with a twinge of both sadness and relief. She could probably survive a few months if she could get her hormones under control.

"Sounds like I'm barely needed at all."

"Oh, quite the contrary." He wiggled his black eyebrows at her suggestively. "I need you. I want you. You are an integral part of this scheme." He playfully sandwiched one of her hands with his own and cradled it gently before releasing it again.

Stephanie shook her head, trying desperately to ignore the tiny flash of heat in her chest at his words and touch.

"You sure you haven't done this before?"

"Absolutely." He reached across the table and took both of her hands into his. Stephanie sobered for a moment and was caught up in the serious expression of his icy eyes that were anything but cold. "Stephanie Von Feldt? Would you please help me con the press and general public into believing that we are a hardcore devoted couple? Then have a fantastic blow-out breakup fight with me in public so everyone knows it's over?" His playfully serious expression was just too much.

"Why, Devon Greene, I would be so honored to charge you a small fortune for providing just such a service."

As Devon planted a gentle kiss on her knuckles, the quiet sound of a camera shutter went off just on the other side of the patio.

"Whoops, spotted." Devon's bright smile faded a bit, then brightened again. "Guess today that guy got lucky. That'll be worth a couple weeks' pay with TMZ."

"I'll never understand why the ones with just a phone don't turn that fake shutter sound off. Seems silly to give yourself away if you've managed to ninja stealth yourself an exclusive picture."

Devon threw his head back in laughter, nodding his agreement.

Momentarily distracted, he tapped out a text to someone after his phone pinged, and glanced around, a half-grin on his face.

"Everything okay?"

"Yeah," he nodded. "Someone from work is giving me a hard time. I think she's around somewhere or drove by or something."

After a few watchful moments, he let it go and they chatted a bit more, his attention split between Stephanie and his phone.

It was silly to feel jealous, but she couldn't help it. Said co-worker was a she, and he was amused by her.

Giving herself a mental slap, Stephanie pushed those thoughts and feelings away and focused on their conversation and her coffee.

Not long after, they finished their drinks and went their separate ways, Stephanie torn between being nervous about spending so much time with Devon all at once with minimal script planning time and being relieved that it would be over before she could make a fool of herself or lose her professional edge.

Who was she kidding—she was already losing her edge. The worst part was that for the first time since she could remember, she actually genuinely got along with a client.

She liked him.

The very idea made her shiver and tingle with long-repressed feelings like *want* and *need*.

Stephanie was in big trouble.

CHAPTER
Six

STEPHANIE WALKED AROUND the pool deck as she waited to see if Maxwell was going to take her call or send her to voice-mail.

It was Thursday afternoon, and there was no telling what he might have on the schedule. He could be doing anything from lounging at the beach in Malibu to sitting in his office being serious and doing his actual job, which the last time they spoke had been some kind of entertainment law.

He would not confirm or deny if he was working as a partner for his father's firm—Hollywood Law—but her money was on yes. He'd always wanted to make partner at Samuel's firm, and she had a feeling he had and just didn't want to celebrate it. Which, if she thought about it too hard, was weird.

Really weird.

She could have texted to see if he was available, but if she didn't just dial, she'd find another reason to put it off. They both did that, and it was maddening, but neither could seem to change.

Three rings.

Four.

Stephanie had begun mentally rehearsing the voice message she would leave when he finally picked up.

"Oh my god, she lives and breathes." Maxwell's warm voice greeted her with a laugh. "And she dates. Devon Greene no less. Are you doing that for real, Lovely? Or are you improving the image of that handsome man for loads of money?"

Stephanie couldn't help but let the wide smile take over her face. Maxwell and she had very few secrets.

"Well, my dearest friend, as I'm sure your father has told you—because I know you asked him weeks ago—there's simply nothing I can say one way or the other on the matter."

Maxwell laughed, and it was a warm sound. It made Stephanie feel like she was getting a full-body hug. She realized then that she really missed seeing her friend.

It was a bit of a surprise, however, how much she realized she had needed that virtual hug. As fiercely independent as she was, feeling lonely or homesick was not something she considered she might feel all that often. With her parents gone, and she and Maxwell doing the thing they always did where they put off calling, she guessed she had started to feel a bit isolated. Surely Devon had helped stave some of that off?

Her attention snapped back to Maxwell.

"—money is on him being a client, but that's none of my business."

"Too right." She paused. "Unless you made partner and know for sure already?"

He laughed again but didn't answer her question. "So? How are things?"

"Things are good. Mom and Dad are taking a slow tour of Europe so I've been staying at their place."

"That's what Pop said. You okay? You sound … funny."

Stephanie gazed across the rippling blue pool.

"Yeah. I'm totally fine!" There was more enthusiasm there than there needed to be. She knew it, and he'd notice for sure. "I'm good. Just busy. And I miss my stuff and my apartment and my canvases."

Maxwell made a thoughtful noise deep in his throat. "I get that. I'd go nuts if I moved back home, no matter if these crazy old people—that I dearly love, don't get me wrong—were around much or not."

Stephanie laughed and they fell into a familiar rhythm, catching up on the things they had missed over past months, promising to do better going forward which usually meant a couple of weeks of check-in texts and maybe a few emails before they fell off altogether again until the next phone call.

"We should have lunch." He suggested.

Stephanie stopped her loping barefoot laps around the pool deck, considering.

"I'm not sure that's a great idea right now. The press has been pretty stuck to me lately."

Maxwell laughed. She realized then that she'd fallen for his trap.

"So, he is a client. I didn't say we'd have to go out, darling." If he were a cartoon villain, he'd be grinning and twirling the ends of his handlebar mustache around his fingers. "I'll come to you? You come to me? Either way. I'd love to see your face."

Stephanie's cheeks heated. Nobody knows you better than a life-long friend.

Jerk.

She smiled and they hashed out tentative plans for the following week.

After she hung up, she sat on the edge of the pool, dipping her feet in the water. It was still chilly on her feet. The April sun hadn't had enough time to help warm the water yet.

A sliver of warmth from her conversation with Maxwell remained in her heart, but she suddenly felt too small surrounded by the gigantic estate. Too alone, too … friendless.

But that was by design, wasn't it? Silly to be mad about a situation you set up for yourself. She shook her head and with a frustrated huff, she got up and went into the pool-house, determined to shake away her doldrums with paint and canvas.

FRIDAY'S DINNER DATE seemed to creep up on Stephanie much quicker than she hoped.

At 6:30 she was still trying to decide which Asian-inspired Diane Von Furstenburg dress she was going to wear. The red wrap dress with the white fan pattern or the sleek black satin with gold and green floral accents at the hem? She tried them both on again. Twice.

Sighing her frustration, she decided to text Devon. It was not like her to miss discussing such an important detail of the plan. She needed to get her head fully in the game, and quick.

S: *How dressy are we going?*

The black was definitely sexier, the red more playful. If this was a serious romantic date, the black would definitely be the one. If this was a fun dinner date, the red was more appropriate. She was mad that she hadn't asked for more details. This was part of date scripting, 101. What the hell was he paying her for if she was going to only partly do her job?

Giving up on the clothing for a moment, Stephanie went into the bathroom to put the finishing touches on her twist up-do which she secured with a gold-accented black clip and her makeup.

Her phone chimed.

D: *Fashion dilemma? Dressy casual. No need to pull out the big guns.*

Stephanie's mouth tugged into a half-grin. "Red it is." She mumbled aloud.

She quickly pulled on the dress, paired it with some white Jimmy Choos and a tiny red clutch purse. Satisfied, she worked on transferring everything she would need for the date into the small bag. Just as she finished, there was a buzz from the gate. Stephanie double checked that it was Devon, then pressed the button to open the barricade.

She swung the heavy front door open just as he was raising a hand to knock.

"Hey." He smiled in greeting. "You look amazing."

"Thanks, so do you." And he did. He had black slacks on and a crisp gray shirt. The shirt made his sharp blue eyes seem even more intense than usual.

A palm to her lower back, Devon guided her to his car after she locked up. Ever the gentleman, he opened her door and she slid in, breathing in the leather and Devon scent of the interior.

Ever since someone had asked her what he smelled like at the salon, Stephanie had been trying to pin it down. It was somewhere between that musky ozone smell just before it rains and the earthy smell just after the first drops fall. It was clean, and comfortable, just like him.

Her back straightened as she realized where her mind had gone. She forced a smile and his gentle one made the tips of her ears burn.

As Devon steered them toward downtown Los Angeles, he tried to get a feel for how the date was going to go. "Your message lined it out, but I'm an audio learner." He gave her that dashing grin again. It was irritatingly irresistible.

"Pretty much like lunch. Maybe some more flamboyant body language, nothing too over the top. Photographers will only see us on the way in and out, but the rest of the dining room will see how we interact." Stephanie pushed herself into Adjuster mode.

Devon nodded. "This really is your day job, isn't it?" His expression was a cross between incredulous and impressed.

"Yes." Stephanie laughed.

"It's weird. You're quite good at it. I keep forgetting."

Stephanie thought that was as good a compliment as she could hope for considering her traitorous mercurial emotions and hormones.

Flashbulbs were blinding in the twilight as they exited the vehicle. As usual, the pair just ignored the ridiculous shouted questions. Giving any response could be completely damning, even if meant as kind or joking.

Devon took Stephanie's hand as the valet palmed his keys and they entered the restaurant with their new-relationship happy smiles in place.

After being seated and ordering, Stephanie sipped at her green tea and kept her face in a peaceful, adoring grin as they spoke. It seemed like it should have taken more effort than it did, but Devon was a genuinely nice guy, easy to talk to and really did have her attention.

Early dates—whether put-on or real—were still about getting to know the other person beyond what they'd put on their dating questionnaire, so that's what they were doing.

"How did you find yourself in this line of work?" Devon asked, making quick work of a pod of edamame. "Didn't you act when you were younger? Why did you stop? You're clearly beautiful, young, and a Von Feldt for crying out loud."

Stephanie nodded, then gave a bit of a shrug as she too used her teeth to coax the soybeans out of their pods.

"I enjoyed it as a kid. I was cute enough to get some work, and of course, being a Von Feldt never hurt." She could feel her eyebrows come together. "I don't know, I just fell out of love with it when I started being shuffled off as the fat friend at casting calls. Nobody likes to hear they aren't leading lady material. It seems to be changing a bit now, but my heart isn't in it."

"The fat friend? That's absurd." Devon looked truly disgusted. "You're gorgeous."

"That's very nice of you to say." Stephanie was truly flattered by his indignation on her behalf and the compliments. "But I'm built like a swimmer, not a model. You know as well as I do I'm not the body-type they are looking for. I'm not tall enough, not willowy enough, have too many muscles and am too broad in the shoulders and hips." She shrugged. There was plenty of time to come to terms with that reality for her. "It's getting better, but honestly I don't want to act as much as I would have to in order to go after the parts. I don't have the energy to play that game. I've got other projects."

Devon gave a gentle nod, eyes conveying his sympathy with her on how crazy and unrealistic that thinking was.

"So, since you're not acting on TV or in the movies…how long have you been doing this?"

Stephanie laughed. She saw what he was trying to do.

"Nope. Sorry. You're not going to get me to tell you how many years I've been in this job or clients I've had. But good try."

Devon looked wounded but was still smiling. "As if I would use that information for nefarious purposes."

"Regardless," Stephanie tossed aside another empty pod after gently scraping out the contents with her teeth. "I'm not falling for it."

"Fine." Devon sighed, leaned back a bit in his seat and regarded her carefully. She hadn't missed the careful way his eyes tracked her mouth and the edamame pod, pupils dilating ever so slightly. It warmed something in her chest. It was never not nice to be wanted. Being the object of someone's desire was a warm, tingly feeling and she welcomed it, even if she shouldn't. Even if he was a client.

"So, if you don't love acting, what do you love? I know you're not dating as a full-time gig. If you were, you'd either have an ugly 'she gets around' label or someone would have caught on and put you out of work by now."

Stephanie gave him a coy grin. He was smart.

"Well thought out, Mr. Greene." She ribbed him. He lowered his lashes in a kind of bow. "I live in another city most of the time. I spend time alone. I read. I paint. I go to the beach. I swim. I'm just an ordinary girl."

"I doubt that, very much." Devon said seriously, that devastating grin on his lips. Stephanie couldn't help but return the smile. It was nice to be flirted with, regardless of the circumstance. Regardless of whether or not it was genuine.

They were interrupted by the waiter delivering the chef's special offering of sushi and sashimi.

"This looks amazing." Stephanie took in the artfully arranged plate of designer seafood rolls with amazement.

"One of my favorite things in the whole world when it comes to food." Devon's eyes glittered as he began to pull pieces from the platter to his plate.

They discussed what it was like for Stephanie to grow up with the Von Feldt power duo as parents, how Devon grew up in a small town in Alabama with devoted parents and three annoying younger brothers, how his foundation was mainly about supporting neglected or abandoned animals and his other charity efforts; of which there were an impressive number. Eventually, they made their way around to discussing the awkward teenage years and then college—Devon lit up like a Christmas tree as he told Stephanie how he'd met his friend Nora in college and how they'd gone through the University of South Alabama's Dramatic arts program together—and how fickle the industry had been to them both.

Devon admitted knowing how very lucky he was to be one of the main characters on a show with a solid following, and that he didn't know if he had it in him to pursue too many other projects when the show finally ended. Hopefully, there were at least a few seasons left before he had to worry about that.

It had felt comfortable and natural to Stephanie, and she was only momentarily nervous that she had forgotten to actually do her job. The organic feel to their chemistry as they talked over a ridiculous amount of sushi and green tea had been much more beneficial than any put-on act she could have conjured up.

Just recognizing that she was letting Devon into her self-imposed bubble made her try to put it back up.

Devon gave a sigh as the waitress cleared the last of their dishes and returned the leather wallet with his credit card receipt inside.

"Well. It was nice while it lasted, right?" he smiled.

"It was. This was a great idea. I don't eat good sushi nearly enough."

Devon gave her an appreciative smile and offered a hand to help her out of the booth. "Please don't tell me you've been eating bad sushi?"

Hand once again on her lower back, Devon guided her out of the restaurant toward the valet stand.

"Definitely not. Bought some at a grocery store one time. That's all it took."

He pulled a face. "I can only imagine."

They blinked their way past all the photographers on their way out, same patient, kind smile painting their lips, same vacant eyes and lack of response to the shouts and questions.

Devon's fingers gently threaded through Stephanie's and she couldn't help but note that their linked fingers were a good fit and his touch was warm and soft. The part of her mind controlling rational thought also noted, and pleasantly, that he was also very carefully keeping to the contract's touch limits.

They were a great match.

For business.

Definitely only for business.

Stephanie felt her cheeks heat and tried to mentally disengage from any wayward romantic thoughts. She vowed to set a boundary that they both understood so that this wouldn't continue. She couldn't let it or she would have to break the contract.

The very idea of that made her sad, made something clench near where her heart should be and that enraged her as well as set her resolve in concrete. In no way did she want a comparison in her mind between Devon Greene and Ollie Parkinson, and a canceled contract would do just that.

The drive home was quiet, a jazzy tune on the stereo filling the somehow not awkward silence.

"That was really nice." Devon smiled and leaned in to kiss Stephanie on the cheek as she got ready to get out of the car and go inside the house.

Stephanie pulled away from him before he could make contact, opened her door and had one leg out before she turned to Devon.

'Nice' was the kiss of death in real relationships. Stephanie wasn't sure how to feel about it in their context, but it looked like she might not be the only one on the cusp of developing real feelings.

That could be really dangerous for everyone and had to be shut down immediately.

"There's nobody watching us here, Devon. I just want you to know it's not necessary to bring me flowers, or compliment my outfit or kiss me goodnight." She had a calm and gentle lift to the corners of her mouth, the essence of a smile, but was quite serious. Stephanie didn't want to start having any more trouble compartmentalizing this job; she didn't want the lines blurred any further by either of them. She could feel this business partnership morphing into a kind of friendship, and crossing that line alone was tempting fate enough.

Devon gave her a soft smile and spoke gently. "I know, Stephanie. Part of it is my very Southern mother beating good manners into me and my brothers, but honestly, I wouldn't say anything to you I didn't mean. You're a beautiful woman. Surely, it's okay for me to tell you so. I'm sorry if trying to kiss you overstepped. I forgot myself for a moment and was just … feeling."

She nodded her head gently, once, heart beating frantically against her ribs. "It's alright. I just wanted you to know that it's not required. There are no bonus points awarded for manners. Though maybe there should be?" She returned his smile and then switched gears. He hadn't spoken much about his family, but it seemed like they were quite close. "Brothers?"

Devon smiled. "Three. I'm the oldest, and most handsome, obviously." The smirk appeared. "They're all bigger than me though. They help run the non-profit foundation we started a few years ago back home. Mom made the mistake of giving us all names that start with D too—it was really rough on her when one of us was in trouble."

Stephanie couldn't help but laugh, picturing that.

"She's a saint though." He smiled. "Good night Stephanie."

"Good night, Devon."

Stephanie went into the dark, empty house feeling like something inside her was burning, and not in a good way. For that night, she tried to ignore the temptation of allowing herself to forge a friendship or any relationship, not business-related with Devon and just tried to enjoy the sensation of being thought beautiful by a devastatingly handsome, intelligent and funny man.

What girl wouldn't?

CHAPTER
Seven

AFTER THEIR SUSHI date, Stephanie had called Devon to the house to go over the nitty-gritty and explain why she was acting the way she was and to get on the same page with him in that regard. To her fortune, he understood and was totally on-board with front-loading for the next few weeks so that there were no surprises.

"I'm sorry if I was being too … familiar." He apologized again; icicle eyes bright as he regarded her carefully over a coffee mug in her parents' living room.

She shook her head and sat across from him on a chaise, picking up pen and notebook after setting her own coffee down on the table between them. The repeated apology struck her as a little funny considering she was in casual jeans and a t-shirt and they were drinking coffee while sitting on sofas where she was living instead of at a neutral public space or even meeting in the office across the house.

"Not at all. It's good that the press got to see that we were comfortable and enjoying ourselves. That's very important to selling this as real. Sometimes it takes a bit of time to figure out what kind of preparations suit best—we were just getting that sorted out." She smiled. He returned it, and she squashed the warm feeling in her stomach as soon as it started to rise.

"I do like to think that we are familiar, Stephanie. Aren't we?"

She regarded him carefully. His attractiveness was a bit devastating this close up. She remembered to breathe; a careful smile painted on her face.

Alarm bells rang loudly in her head. Alert! Alert! FEELINGS. REAL ONES. Warning! She shook her head, trying to clear her thoughts. She had a mental picture of the emotions from Inside Out running around in her head.

"Of course. I'd say even a bit friendly, wouldn't you?"

He beamed. "Absolutely."

"Good. Now shall we schedule out the next few weeks in painful detail? Down to the very last held hand and cheek kiss?"

He laughed, and it felt much like Maxwell's had as it embraced her. Just not brotherly like Maxwell's. Not brotherly at all.

The feeling that she was in seriously deep shit did not subside.

After Devon left nearly three hours later, they had two weeks' worth of dates mapped out in excruciatingly scripted detail, the schedule sent both to Devon's people as well as to Marty. Stephanie felt better about her ability to be professional since she had no way to not be prepared for their outings.

They would be going to coffee and restaurants, exploring museums together, even making a day of Disneyland. Stephanie had even suggested she venture out and visit Devon on set. They found each other easy to talk to, fun to be around and that was as good a situation as one could ask for in their business arrangement.

As she was loading the dishwasher the buzzer at the driveway gate buzzed. She wondered if Devon had maybe forgotten something, but she saw on the monitor that it was Maxwell. Her surprise quickly melted into excitement as she pressed the button to allow his flashy red Mercedes Roadster entry.

Her legs carried her quickly down the hall to the front door and she was able to open it before he was even out of the car.

"Have you missed me that much?" he laughed, opening his arms wide.

Stephanie jogged down the steps and threw herself into his embrace. She wrapped her arms around him like a sloth around a branch and held tight. Because of their height difference, mostly she was clinging to his ribs, but it didn't matter. He folded all of his expansive wing-span around her and she took a deep, steadying breath. After a long moment, she let go, and he pulled her back to arms-length from him.

"Actually, yes, I did." She admitted, diving in for one more quick hug.

"You'll inflate my already devastatingly large ego saying things like that, Alex." Maxwell winked at her and pulled away, gathering some bags from the passenger side of the car.

He was the only one who ever called her that, and she loved it.

When she was younger, she had hated the name Stephanie. Despised the way it sounded like a pink and sparkles all the time girl name. She had demanded she be called Alex for a few months when she was eleven. Her mother outright refused to go along with it, her father found it amusing for a little while. Maxwell thought it was much more appropriate than Stephanie and never quit.

"Don't I know it. What did you bring me?"

He laughed and held up the bags for her inspection.

"What kind of friend would I be if I hadn't stopped at Mr. Woo's on my way over?"

Stephanie's stomach gave a bit of a rumble. Mr. Woo's was her favorite and Maxwell knew it.

"A horrible one."

She led him back into the house, helping unpack what looked like enough food for a whole house full of people onto the kitchen island.

"Are we having more company?" She joked, getting out plates and silverware.

"No, why?" His expression was so serious Stephanie couldn't help but laugh again.

"No reason."

They loaded their plates and settled to eat at the small dinette in the breakfast area.

"I thought we weren't meeting until Thursday?" Stephanie said around a mouthful of lo-mein.

Maxwell shrugged. "You said this evening was free and I had a craving for egg rolls."

She narrowed her eyes at him. "That's it?"

He stared at her, and very slowly, she saw pink color his cheeks. "I do miss you, Alex. And I do love Mr. Woo's eggrolls."

She set her chopsticks down. "But?"

Maxwell did that lopsided grin thing that only men seem to be able to do and make it seem sexy. Stephanie was pretty sure she'd look like a lunatic if she tried.

"But… Dad—and Marty—wanted me to check on you. They worry about you being here by yourself."

Stephanie sighed and felt her affection for the kooky old men grow three sizes.

"I'm a grown-up, Maxwell. An adult. I do lots of… adulty things, all on my own."

He chuckled and ate an entire eggroll in two bites. "I know." He mumbled around it. After a moment of chewing and a quick wipe with a napkin, he continued. "But I wanted to see you anyway. It just worked out."

Stephanie stabbed at a dumpling.

"Well, you can tell your dad that everything is just fine. Marty too. Just like I have been, every time he calls me to check-in."

"I will." He nodded, a broad grin on his face.

Stephanie watched him. He was hiding something.

"What else, Maxwell? What aren't you telling me, you terrible, terrible liar."

He burst out laughing then, as though keeping it in had been painful.

"I ran into that guy on my way in. Devon, right? He was coming out of the gate as I pulled in the drive. Pretty sure he's going to want to know why you have a dinner date. I may have mentioned something about staying over, too."

Stephanie felt her mouth hang open and something sink in her stomach.

"You what?"

"He's into you. Client or not, he likes you Alex. I'm fairly certain he wanted to ask me to get out of the car and punch me in the face." He stared at her for a moment, an impossibly adorable smirk on his face. "He didn't though, he was all class. Just smiled and said he hoped we'd get a chance to meet each other properly one day soon."

Stephanie tossed a pot-sticker directly at his face. It bounced off his forehead and he managed to catch it in one meaty hand. Then, he ate it.

"I can't believe you! What's the matter with you?" But she wasn't mad, she realized. She was laughing. And it was a foreign feeling that she realized she needed a lot more of.

That was Maxwell. He was a gigantic 12-year-old and she needed more of that playfulness in her life.

"So, can I sleep over?" He asked innocently.

She lobbed another pot-sticker but nodded.

"Of course you can. You know mom keeps that room ready just for you."

He gave that easy grin and she couldn't help but smile. It was really too bad they were out of foods she could easily throw at his adorably annoying face.

AN ACTION FLICK, a chick flick and two terrible horror movies plus a ridiculous amount of the Chinese food and a batch of popcorn later, Stephanie found herself close to falling asleep on the couch.

Maxwell was stretched out on the other end of the sectional, a pile of pillows surrounding him. Stephanie had gathered a few for herself before he could take them all and was propped up on her side, covered in her mother's favorite cashmere throw. Her eyes felt gritty as she blinked at the credits rolling across the screen.

"I'm done, Max. You?"

He stretched his arms above his head, a giant yawn keeping him from responding. Finally, a nod.

"Yeah. Thanks for letting me stay. I really don't want to get in the car."

Stephanie pulled off the blanket and turned off the TV.

"Come on then, you know where your room is."

"I do." He agreed, following her through the dimly lit halls toward the guest room that was a few doors down from her own bedroom.

She made sure the guest suite was ready and the bathroom stocked (but really, between the housekeeper and her mother she shouldn't have even thought it would be an issue,) before throwing her arms around Maxwell one more time.

"Thank you." She mumbled into his chest. His stature rivaled Alan's minus some bulk.

His arms were firm bands as he squeezed her.

"My pleasure, darling." He just held her like that for a moment. "You know you don't have to do this isolation thing, right? You can make other friends? It's a somewhat adulty thing to do."

She stepped back and looked him in the eye. He was rarely so sanguine. His chocolate eyes regarded her with deep affection and worry.

"I'm fine, Maxwell. Friends are overrated—unless they're you of course."

He sighed. "Not all girls are like them, Alex. Not all girls—"

"And not all guys are like him, Max. I know. I don't have time for a big group of friends, anyway. I don't even live here anymore." She'd be damned if she was going to say her ex's name.

His expression softened.

"Yeah, I know. But you could make friends there too." He broke eye contact and pulled the duvet back from the pillows on the bed. "I love you Alex. You're the bratty little sister I always wanted but didn't want to have live with me all the time. I just want to be sure you're happy. I'm not around much, your parents are globe-trotting and you pretend date for a living. That seems pretty lonely."

Her breath started to crawl into her lungs sharply, but she turned it into a heavy sigh. "I love you too, Max. I'm really okay, I swear. And you're not responsible for making sure I'm not lonely, you know." It all felt a little bit like a lie as she said it, but she brushed past that. A thought occurred to her. "Will Olivia be upset that you're here?"

Maxwell laughed. "I doubt it. She's likely staying over with James."

"Oh. I'm sorry." She wasn't really. Olivia was an awful girlfriend and a pretty terrible human being. Also, a massive bitch. She liked to toy with Maxwell constantly and Stephanie couldn't stand her. She'd be an excellent match for Ollie Parkinson, come to think of it. "When did that happen?"

"Don't fret, sweet Alex. I know you didn't care for her. That was quite a while ago and I'm not even a bit broken up about it. I knew it would only be good while it lasted. And it wasn't even really that good if I'm being honest."

She gave a watery smile and made her way to the door. "You're not like those girls or him either, Max. Quit trying to convince me you are. You're a giant teddy bear. The right girl is going to come along one day, I just know it. You won't know what hit you. But I will."

He smiled that broad, bright smile she knew brought most girls to their knees. That smile always seemed much more suited to a surfer than a lawyer, but she supposed it all worked out.

"If you say so, Alex."

He didn't seem averse to the idea, she noted, which was very interesting indeed.

"Sleep well. If you're nice maybe I'll make us brunch." She offered.

He laughed and tossed his watch to the nightstand with a heavy clank.

"Isn't that a Rolex?" She teased, mock horrified. He just smirked in response.

"I'm always nice. And why not breakfast?"

"I'm sleeping in. I trust you can figure out the coffee pot if you're up before me."

He laughed softly and nodded. "You bet. I'm ridiculously handy like that. At least when it comes to my caffeine."

"Goodnight my favorite pain in the ass friend."

"Goodnight, Alex, my lovely weirdo friend."

IT WAS DEFINITELY more brunch than breakfast when Stephanie wandered into the kitchen to find Maxwell tucked into a cup of coffee, looking perfectly spotless. He'd recently showered and his clothes were clean and unwrinkled. Had he brought a bag she didn't notice? For all she knew, he kept a couple of changes of clothes in the guest room closet. Honestly, that option made lots of sense. The clothes would be a bit out of season, but still usable.

"There she is." He smiled at her, flipping pages in her father's daily LA Times.

"Where?" Stephanie joked, looking over her shoulder.

"Har, har."

She smiled as she poured herself a cup of coffee and doctored it up the way she liked.

"Bacon or sausage?" She quizzed.

He looked affronted.

"*Bacon*. Who even are you that you're asking me that question?"

"My apologies Your Majesty." She held her hands up in surrender and began to dig out the makings for French toast. There was nothing better than baked French toast in her opinion.

"No, but seriously, who are you hanging out with that there's a choice other than bacon?"

Stephanie just wiggled her eyebrows at him as she separated the strips and placed them on a baking sheet.

Once the bacon and French toast were both in the oven, she slid into a chair across from him.

"Sleep okay?"

"Definitely. I even took a picture of the mattress label."

Stephanie laughed. "I'm glad."

It was nice, sitting in comfortable silence with Maxwell, drinking coffee and scanning the paper, then eating brunch. He was very low maintenance, despite his flashy car and Rolex. They had been friends since forever, and just being in the same room was enough.

After helping clean up the dishes, Maxwell dropped a kiss in her hair and regrettably said he had to get going.

"I'm behind on work and I have to get caught up before Monday."

"I understand. I need to get rested for my busy relationship schedule."

Maxwell boomed with laughter. "Hopefully you're able to smooth things over with him. Sorry if I caused a problem, Alex."

"No, you're not." Stephanie laughed, watching as he opened his car door.

"You're right, I'm not." His light brown hair glowed with blonde streaks in the sunshine. The smirk on his face could give Devon's a solid run for its money.

"I know." She just watched him for a moment longer. "Miss you, Max. We need to not suck at this quite so badly. But I love hanging out with you."

"Same here, Lovely. I'll call you soon."

"Sure, you will." Stephanie winked at him and could hear his laughter as he climbed into the little roadster and pulled away from the house with a wave.

She stood there a few moments, reveling in the sensation that her batteries had been recharged before returning to the house and getting ready for her upcoming week.

A QUICK STOP at the grocery store a couple of hours later left her feeling a little off balance once again.

She was in the frozen foods aisle when she heard his voice. And then a laugh that was very female.

Stephanie turned away from the frozen fruit to see Devon and a willowy wisp of a woman laughing their way toward her. Devon's eyes met hers, and she forced a smile. This was not a planned meeting and there was no telling who might be watching.

Devon, always suave, made sure there was no stumbling in the event there were cameras about. He left his friend's side and came to Stephanie, kissing her cheek.

"I didn't expect to see you today. What a pleasant turn of events." He said, a broad smile on his face. The woman with him was smiling also and extended a hand to Stephanie.

"Hi, I'm Nora."

"Hi. Nice to meet you." Stephanie managed to smile and take the girl's graceful fingers into her own hand to shake.

"I'm so glad to finally meet you! Devon has told me so much about you."

"How nice!" Stephanie managed, her brain tickling that she knew this woman from somewhere and just couldn't place her. "I'm sorry, but I feel like we've met before. I feel terrible that I can't recall."

Devon placed a hand comfortably at Stephanie's lower back, and it felt as though he were somehow staking a claim on her as well as giving definition to how he felt about her versus how he felt about Nora. It was excellent use of outlined permitted body language.

"This is the Nora I'm on set with all the time, Steph. She's my co-star and BFF." He smiled. Only someone as handsome and charming as him could refer to someone as his BFF and have it not be totally laughable.

"That must be it! I'm so sorry, I don't get a chance to watch much TV."

Nora laughed again, and it was a sparkly, friendly sound.

"No worries at all. I don't really watch anything either. But I think maybe we also go to the same salon? Do you see Janice?"

It clicked in Stephanie's brain then. The slender woman who had been getting her nails done that day in the salon had been Nora.

"Yes! I recognize you now. I saw you the last time I was there." She thought back. "I'm definitely going to get yelled at if I don't make an appointment soon, too."

Nora smiled broadly. "Janice does not mess around with upkeep."

Devon seemed content and amused to watch them talk.

"I'm so glad we ran into you," he said. "How was your dinner with your … friend?" His expression was pointedly neutral.

Stephanie's gut tightened.

"It was great. I haven't seen Maxwell in quite some time. He's the friend I was telling you about that I've known since we were like five." She explained, even though she couldn't recall ever mentioning Maxwell. Maybe over sushi? No. She didn't think her friends or lack thereof had ever come up.

"I wish I'd had a chance to say hello more than through my car window. Next time." Devon smiled and his thumb began to make circles at her waist. The sensation tingled nerves clear down to her toes.

"Absolutely. Maybe we can all get together soon? I think Maxwell would love to meet you." She looked from Devon's somehow warm ice-blue gaze to Nora. "And you, certainly."

Nora smiled. She was adorable and sweet. It made Stephanie suspicious and that made her frustrated with herself. "I'm always interested in meeting new people."

There was a lull and Devon saved it again by swooping in for a quick but surprisingly thorough mouth kiss that left Stephanie a bit breathless and struggling to push herself back into her Image Adjuster box.

"Sorry to smooch and run, but we've got to get back. I'm really glad this happened." Devon smiled warmly at

Stephanie and she felt a real smile form on her lips. Her insides were quite confused about what part of this was pretend right now.

Nora was all smiles and waved as they went further into the store. She made her pizza selection and headed to the checkout.

Stephanie had no idea how to feel about any of what had happened and thinking about it just made it worse. Once she got home, she tried to shake off the strangeness by going over their calendar and planning outfits and immersing herself in her role—anything and everything she could to push herself back into that safe, stringent, 'work' box.

Eventually, she gave up, went for a long swim and then ended up painting well into the night in the pool-house.

CHAPTER

O VER THE NEXT couple of weeks, as per their very carefully plotted schedule, the pair was busy and spotted all over the place and the highlight of any number of entertainment show gossip.

While getting out in the world and enjoying some great attractions, Stephanie constantly reminded herself that she was on that invisible stage and tried very hard to keep herself contained in her Image Adjuster box, now with reinforced concrete walls.

She liked to think it was concrete, anyway. Some days it felt more like a soap bubble, prone to burst with the tiniest bit of prodding.

She had Marty call in friendlies from the press corps to take and distribute the best photos of Stephanie and Devon together. Devon's publicity team also pitched in to spread the juiciest photos far and wide.

Between them, they had scripted a dozen public kisses—all varying levels of romance and libido enhancing qualities—and two minor spats.

At coffee, they held hands on the tabletop and gave sweet pecks over their lattes. At the museum, they took a break in the great hall of gems and were spotted in a closed-eye open-mouthed kiss that had the tabloids speculating and gossiping.

A trip to Disneyland brought out the playful side of them both and they worked in a whole series of photos involving the characters—Devon smooching Cinderella's cheek, Stephanie being wooed by Prince Charming, Devon dancing with Belle, Stephanie threatening Flynn Ryder with a cast iron skillet—and ending with them in a very Disney kiss themselves.

There was a quick lunch at a 50's style diner that ended early because of a spat over Devon's attention to the adorable waitress and her abundant cleavage and a very public disagreement at a fancy steakhouse over Devon leaving Stephanie waiting alone at their table for nearly 30 minutes while he dallied in the bar trying to get an update on some kind of sporting event.

They were expertly feeding the media's gossip mill and cultivating the environment needed for the big blowout ending.

The attention level on Stephanie was much more than it had been in years if she were to make a guess. She tried not to keep up with the tabloids if she could avoid it—that's what she paid Marty for.

There was much speculation about whether or not she was really as squeaky clean as her image portrayed and lots of joking about what that probably translated to in bed. The general consensus was that it likely meant she was a wildcat, but some argued that she might be just as boring as her good-girl history.

It was definitely an odd thing to watch being debated about yourself on television.

For the most part, Stephanie tried to ignore the shows and the chatter, and just do her job. No real feelings. Just acting.

It was getting harder and that frustrated her. Emotions were much safer to manage if they weren't real.

Devon predicted that week seven of their wild ride relationship would be the time to end it. She couldn't help but lament that she'd prepared and planned for six whole months with him, and she would only end up getting two.

"Sweeps will be the following week. If we plan to have it out in a parking lot after a tense dinner or something with all the paparazzi already hanging around it will be like gold." Devon plotted enthusiastically one afternoon over gelato as they ran errands together. He rubbed his hands together and smirked like a cartoon villain plotting the demise of his nemesis.

The afternoon was part of the script but allowed them to get their shopping done at least. This was the trickiest for Stephanie—when life overlapped the script in a genuine way.

Stephanie nodded and licked a drip of luscious Dutch chocolate gelato off of her finger. "Sounds perfect. Careful, you might be setting yourself up for a new line of work. Just don't put me out of business, okay?" She winked at him. Inside, she was screaming a little. Smiling to cover the other emotions trying to bubble up and expose themselves.

"Wouldn't dream of it. Maybe we could be partners?" He slung his arm around her shoulder and planted a cold kiss on her temple before reaching over to take a taste of her chocolate and offering her a lick of his cappuccino flavored cone.

Partners.

Now there was an idea. Stephanie had to admit that there was definitely something attractive there. What would his definition of that be? She knew hers would be quite multi-faceted given permission to go down that path.

There were a few photographers trying to be inconspicuous, but the pair knew they were lurking about, and were, in fact, counting on it. Magazines and gossip websites and tabloid tv shows were now all running daily updates on their relationship.

Devon had gotten word from his publicist that ratings were up and he was, in fact, in negotiations for a sizeable per episode raise because of his efforts. Stephanie had tried to contain her glee that once again she'd done what she'd set out to do with a client when Devon relayed the news. He, on the other hand, hand been one giant smile and offered to take her to the new dessert bar that specialized in all things chocolate. Of course, they'd gone, how could they not? And that outing had turned that into some great publicity too.

They finished their frozen treats and ambled through a grocery store. The playfulness was real, and they had found themselves becoming actual friends over the last few weeks.

Stephanie had found a reasonable way to balance staying friendly but within the confines of business-like. She was sorely lacking for actual friends, and the waters were always muddy when acting like someone's girlfriend was your job. While uncomfortable, she was trying to find a happy medium between soap bubble and concrete box. For the moment, it was working.

"Ready? We need a good one for the photogs to carry them through the weekend. I'm headed out of town to see my folks and brothers. Have a few things I need to handle in person with the foundation. Won't be back until next Tuesday." Devon closed the rear hatch of the Land Rover Stephanie had driven to the store.

Casually he placed his arms on her shoulders, her hands on his waist, their eyes engaged in what appeared to be an absolutely infatuated gaze.

"Ready as I'll ever be." Stephanie smiled and lifted herself onto her tip-toes to get closer to him.

It was beautiful, as such things go. Excellently executed. Just the right amount of head tilt, some amazingly realistic lip-biting, and tongue work. They could hear the snaps of cameras going off and she could swear there was a chorus of 'oooooh!' in the background.

Stephanie's mind hovered somewhere between that place where the motions of the kiss are remembered like dance steps and the place where she wanted something like this to happen in her real life.

Something moved deep in her chest, like a rusty hinge giving way. She was assuming greatly, but it felt like Devon found his mind much the same place; torn between the strange empty space where he went to do love-scenes for the camera and feeling her warm mouth and breath mingling with his in a very real way. She dared to believe that thinking that way was more than just hope while at the same time whole-heartedly denying wanting that.

When they broke apart, Devon gave her that dreamy enamored grin. "Well done."

She smiled back at him. "And you. Safe travels, okay?"

Finishing off their successful day of acting, he kissed her forehead, lightly holding her face in his hands.

"Always. See you Tuesday."

They let go of one another and Stephanie waved as she got into her father's Land Rover and drove away. The paparazzi were far more interested in Devon than Stephanie that day, and most followed him to his car, some of them shouting questions and snapping shots of him as he got into the driver's seat—it was warm enough that he had put the top down—and with a friendly smile and wave, drove away.

The handful that had stayed back to lob questions at her and get up close and personal shots were rewarded with a smile, a wave and most generously, being allowed to move out of the way before she navigated the SUV out of the parking space.

AS STEPHANIE PUT her groceries away in the impossibly beautiful kitchen that she felt was entirely underused while her parents were gone, the phone rang.

She plucked the extension from the wall by the fridge. Who called a landline anymore?

"Hello?"

"Hey, Kid! How's it going? I see the gig with Mr. Greene is working out."

"Hi, Marty." She shook her head. Of course, it was her agent. The guy who still used fax regularly naturally would call her parents' landline and not her cell phone. "Yes, things seem to be going quite well, don't they?" She pulled a back of pretzels from her last bag of groceries and opened them, snacking while she talked.

"You're like a lucky charm, kid. His PR team called today and the show's ratings are through the roof right now."

"He mentioned something about that. Can't take all the credit, Marty. He's actually really good at this fake relationship thing. We're having a good time." Stephanie crunched a pretzel stick, elbows leaning on the granite-topped island.

"That's good, kid. His people said something about being done around sweeps? I just want to confirm before I do up all the exit paperwork."

Something about the phrase 'exit paperwork' made Stephanie frown. It made it real that their pretend dating life would be ending soon. She shook her head, feeling ridiculous.

"That's what I heard too, Marty. I think you're safe to do the papers."

"Alright kid, you got it. We looking for another guy?"

"I'm not sure, Marty. Don't want it to seem like I'm rebounding or anything, right?"

Marty laughed, a dry guffaw that brought a broad smile to Stephanie's face.

"Sure thing. Talk to you soon, okay? Take care of yourself kid."

"I will Marty, you too." Stephanie was shaking her head as she hung up the phone. Good lord, she loved that crazy man.

After wandering around the house for a solid hour, at a loss for how to entertain herself, she ended up in the pool. She swam laps until she felt like lead weights were in her shoulders and legs and then just floated around in the crystalline blue water, the air around her chilling as the sun began to set.

The horizon was glowing orange when she finally pulled herself out of the water, bundled into a towel and went inside to change.

Stephanie crawled into some yoga pants and a t-shirt, heated some leftover soup and tucked herself into the elaborate sectional couch, losing herself in an edgy, dark psychological thriller before falling into a fitful sleep on the sofa.

THE NEXT MORNING, Stephanie ventured out to the pool-house, throwing the doors and windows open wide to let in the sunshine and some fresh air.

Ever since Stephanie was a child, the pool-house had mainly been used as a studio of some sort. One room had been turned into a dance and martial arts practice area when she was a pre-teen, another room her personal haven in the form of an art studio. Most of her supplies had moved out with her when she had left, but there were still some canvasses and brushes and paints lurking in the room. Once her fingers had organized her remaining brushes and paints, she couldn't stop herself from applying pigment to canvas. It was very nearly a compulsion and something she hadn't indulged in nearly enough since coming to house-sit for her parents, not to mention taking on Devon as a client.

She filled her days with painting while Devon was out of town and she had nothing else to do, the act making her feel centered and complete and grounded in her world. It was the one practice she didn't talk about with anyone, though her parents and even Maxwell knew she was very talented and Stephanie's works graced numerous celebrity homes and even the walls of some notable restaurants and hotel lobbies.

Twice she ventured into the city to purchase more supplies, thinking that it might not be a bad idea to keep a whole other set of her favorite tools in the pool house from now on; especially if her parents were going to continue to travel and she was going to continue to take contracts for a while.

On the second trip, she ran into Nora in the parking lot of the art supply store.

"Stephanie, hi!" Nora said brightly as she approached.

Stephanie closed the rear hatch on the Land Rover and turned with a smile. "Hi, Nora. How are you?"

Nora smiled. "I'm good." She looked a bit uncomfortable as they stood there looking at one another. "This is weird, right? Trying to make friends as grown-ups?"

Stephanie looked at her for a moment and then burst out laughing. She wasn't wrong.

"Yes. Stupid hard. Would you like to get a coffee or something?"

Nora lit up. "Yes. Please."

They bundled off to the local chain and made small talk over their drinks.

"I don't have many friends." Nora admitted almost shyly, her stick-straight blonde hair falling over her shoulders as she dipped to sip her hot drink.

"Me neither." Stephanie smiled at her. "I haven't in a long time. It's hard to know who's really your friend around here."

Nora nodded, wide-eyed. Stephanie noted that Nora's eyes were somewhere between her own warm brandy tone and Maxwell's deep chocolate color. It was a lovely shade, really. "Exactly. Devon's like one of three people on set who is actually a nice person. Everyone else will act like your friend but would push you in front of a bus if it meant more screen time. And it's weird to count him since we've been friends so long."

Stephanie chuckled.

"That's hard. But he is pretty great." Stephanie's smile was genuine, and it warmed her chest better than the hot coffee.

"He is." Nora nodded. "And you guys are just the cutest together. I didn't mean to be eavesdropping that day in the salon, but he was already talking about you on set and just being adorable." She beamed.

Stephanie felt her head tilt. "Really? That was so early. We'd barely met! Not that we've been together all that long now, but…"

"But you guys are great together." Nora smiled in a romantic, moony kind of way. "I'm really happy for him. Did you know we went to college together?"

Stephanie felt surprise move through her body. "No. How fun that you got to reconnect on a job though."

"It was such a lucky thing. I was so glad to see him again! I had such a crush on him freshman year."

Something must have shifted in Stephanie's expression. Nora quickly raised her hands.

"No, no. Please don't think that I still do. No way. Devon and I … we're much better as friends. He's gorgeous, but we are like brother and sister."

Stephanie nodded. "I get that. Maxwell and I are like that."

Nora smiled again and took a big drink of her latte. "Maxwell? I think you mentioned him when we ran into one another at the store the other day."

Stephanie nodded. "My best friend. I've known him all my life. I'm sure our parents—also friends since forever—once thought we might end up together but we aren't romantic at all. Same deal. Brother from another mother. Love him, but not like that."

Nora's pixie-like visage was beaming. "Exactly like that. Maybe I'll meet him one day."

Stephanie nodded, mentally calculating Nora and Maxwell's compatibility. It checked out, actually, and she filed that information away for another day.

They sat there for a few minutes, drinking their coffees and a bit awkwardly trying to figure out next steps.

"I don't know how to say this without it sounding like I'm hitting on you, but can I have your number? Maybe I can text you some time or we can go to coffee like this now and then? It would be nice to have a friend that isn't someone I work with and isn't a dude." Nora said.

Stephanie smiled. It would be complicated. She and Devon would both be lying to her which seemed totally unkind and unfair. Stephanie's guard would have to be up basically all the time so she didn't slip. The media would surely start creating stories about Nora and Stephanie and probably Nora and Devon… and likely Nora and Stephanie and Devon. But…

She could hear Maxwell in the back of her mind, reminding her that not all girls were like the friends she used to have.

"That would be really nice, I think." And it would, Stephanie realized. It really, really would.

The sun was jealous of the rays coming off of the smile those words produced in Nora.

The women exchanged phone numbers and finished their drinks surrounded by friendly chatter.

All the way home Stephanie reveled in the feeling that she had done something brave, and something good. It really would be nice to have another friend.

MONDAY NIGHT STEPHANIE felt a strange mix of exhaustion and accomplishment. She had completed two new pieces, but she had stayed up most of the night Saturday and Sunday, napping in the pool-house bedroom only when she couldn't keep her eyes open any longer. Carefully she washed off the multitude of paint smears all over her hands, forearms and even her face and feet, scrubbing away the aqua and azure and crimson in the nearly scalding water, the act both cathartic and reminiscent of closure.

Stephanie called out for pizza, eating seated at the island in the kitchen. The house felt too big, too cavernous, too cold and empty. Once she had stored her leftovers in the fridge, she tried to lose herself in some mindless television but didn't have any luck. She gave up, locked up the main house and went back to the pool-house, deciding that a night swim would loosen up the shoulders that were tight from three days spent painting.

Not wanting to go back to retrieve a suit, Stephanie stripped down to nothing and went skinny dipping in her parents' pool. The neighborhood was secure enough she didn't really worry about paparazzi peeking over the hedges at her, but the threat of such a thing sped her heart-rate up as she slipped through the barely warm water, the feel of it sliding over and around her verging on sensual.

As much as she hated to admit it, Stephanie needed to get laid. Or something. She needed real affection and touch in her life that wasn't attached to a contract and wasn't platonic.

She went back and forth, the whole length of the pool until she was nearly numb, hauled herself out of and loped into the pool-house where she rinsed off, pulled on a t-shirt and then went to sleep on the sofa, virtually unaware that a re-run of Devon's show was on in the background.

CHAPTER
Nine

THE SOUND OF her phone chiming woke Stephanie the next morning. The TV was still on, only now it was some infomercial for kitchen gadgets on the screen. She shut it off before digging around in the pile of blankets on the couch to find her cell phone.

D: *Feel like pancakes?*

The text made Stephanie warm from head to toe and smile brightly.

S: *Sure. Where?*

She scrubbed some of the sleep from her face and started the shower in the expansive open spa bathroom.

D: *Blu Jam? In an hour?*

S: *Sounds good.*

Stephanie showered and wrapped herself in a towel, feeling ridiculous and even more disconnected from her parents' home as she locked up the pool-house to go get dressed in the main house.

Breakfast on a Tuesday surely only called for some vintage Levi 501 jeans and a swanky vintage Beatles t-shirt, she thought. She left her hair mostly wild but up in a high ponytail, a soft curl to it since she didn't do anything but let it air dry.

Stephanie realized there was an extra bounce in her step and tried to rationalize that it was because she was finally getting out of the house. After all, she was going to breakfast with a friend. That was a perfectly acceptable reason to feel happy. Pancakes could always be counted on to bring a smile, right?

She pulled into the parking lot of the restaurant to see that the paparazzi had been tipped off well. There were no fewer than two dozen men and women with giant cameras snapping photos as she got out of her car. Devon pulled in twenty seconds after she did, and the team of photogs got plenty of fodder as he flashed her that devastating smile, pulled her in close and laid a big, fat smooch right on her mouth.

As he wrapped an arm around her shoulders and steered her into the restaurant he whispered into her ear. "Missed you. You miss me?"

Stephanie laughed, but she could feel herself heating up and the blush rose quickly into her cheeks. He was truly getting better at this game than she had ever been.

"Naturally. My life was void of light and laughter while you were gone."

He made a perfect O of his mouth. "Oooh, I like that."

They were seated near the windows, so they would effectively be on camera their entire meal. That was a bit of a downer, but a hazard of the profession.

"What'll it be?" A kind-faced older woman was their waitress. She reminded Stephanie of her mother's sister June. She planned to leave the woman, Frances, by her nametag, a large tip just because of the resemblance.

"Has to be the crunchy French toast." Stephanie smiled.

Devon raised his eyebrows in an 'oh, really?' kind of expression.

"Breakfast Trio with pancakes for me. Eggs scrambled light, please."

Frances winked at them as she took their menus. "You got it." She swooped back in with coffee and then was off in a breath of Old Lace perfume.

"She's great. I get her section every single time I come in here." Devon said a grin on his face.

"How was your trip? Your mom doing okay? Everything good at the foundation?" Stephanie asked, stirring a packet of raw sugar and a dollop of half and half into her coffee.

Devon gave a lazy smile. "She's fantastic, as usual.

Always reminds me who I am, you know? I can't get away with anything when she's around."

Stephanie laughed. "Only kind of."

"Right, Hollywood royalty parents." He shrugged. "Well you would never know it, so that's a huge credit to them and to you. They raised you right. Or at least that's what my mother would say about it." He sipped at his coffee; icy blue eyes playful over the rim of his mug.

"They would be flattered, thanks." Stephanie made a mental note to remember to tell her parents what he had said. They really would appreciate the compliment it was meant to be.

Frances dipped in with their breakfasts. "Can I get you anything else?"

"No, ma'am, this is perfect." Devon gave her a heart-melting smile.

Frances beamed at him. "Alright. You kids enjoy."

"What about the foundation—was there some kind of problem?"

Devon shook his head. "No, not really. My brothers had what amounted to a development proposition for me. I just need to see it, approve and sign off. It means growth, a bit uncomfortable and with a new set of challenges, but the good kind."

"That's good." She set about cutting her French toast into bite-sized pieces. "Wait. Brothers? How many? Do they look like you?" she feigned interest as she needled him.

She remembered that he'd told her about them before, but it was just too good an opportunity to tease him.

Devon pretended to look scandalized. "That's just cold."

On a laugh, Stephanie lifted her fork and closed her eyes to enjoy the first bite in all its perfection. It had been entirely too long since she had treated herself to the explosion of delicious perfection that was the French toast and vanilla bean sauce.

"Oh. My. God." She heard Devon rumble quietly, but with emphasis.

Eyes still closed, slightly annoyed that her first-bite-worship had been interrupted, she mumbled, "What's wrong?"

"Nothing, nothing at all." The booth creaked as he shifted around in his seat.

When she opened her eyes, he had a perfectly predatory grin on his face, eyes fixed on hers, his hands steepled under his chin.

"Seriously, what?" She demanded, a short nervous laugh escaping her lips. "You look like the cat that ate the canary."

He finally took his fork in hand and took a bite of his pancakes.

"It's nothing, really." He said, swinging the fork around for emphasis as he chewed. "It's just now I know exactly what your O face looks like."

Stephanie blinked at him, feeling the heat rise into her cheeks, and annoyingly into other, much lower places.

"Excuse me?"

"You know. The face you make when you—"

"Yes, I'm quite aware of what you're referring to." She blushed furiously, his flirty grin and playful eyes only making it worse.

Those reinforced Image Adjuster walls were crumbled into dust. The bubble popped into a splatter of soap.

Shit.

"You made it just now, is all." He inhaled another massive bite of fluffy pancakes and smiled at her while he chewed.

"No, I most certainly did not. That was a … a foodgasm you saw. Perfectly delectable first bite worship—which you totally interrupted by the way, rude. Definitely a different thing." She quipped, attempting to recover their lighthearted banter and tingling all over. This was flirting. Real flirting, and she wasn't prepared for the feels.

He laughed broadly, the rich warm sound filling the space between them and filling her heart with gladness. She wasn't even annoyed to see the photographers basically staring at them through the window at that moment.

"You're amazing, Stephanie Von Feldt. Never a dull moment with you. I'm glad we got to know each other."

He smiled and lowered his voice as he said the last, and she returned the warm expression he was giving her.

"Me too, Mr. Greene."

It was by far the best breakfast ever spent with paparazzi capturing every single open-mouthed moment on the other side of a thin pane of glass.

CHAPTER
Ten

STEPHANIE WAS A torrent of emotions. Somehow, it had already become week seven and she was getting dressed for a movie premiere that would double as the public break-up extravaganza locale. A huge blowout breakup fight on the red carpet before a movie premiere? What could be better?

Frustrated with her frizzing hair, she tossed the clip she had been trying to use into the sink, where it broke into three chunks of plastic and the spring flew across the room into the tub. She blew out a breath and leaned her hands on the marble counter-top.

"Get it together." She whispered to herself. After a few deep breaths, she located a different clip, wrangled her chocolate hair into a French twist and finished her makeup, highlighting her light brown eyes with bronze and rich mahogany eye-shadows to dramatic effect.

The last two weeks had been a frenzy of activity after their highly photographed and publicized breakfast date. They staged three more spats of varying degrees of ugliness and kept their public displays of affection to stiff cheek kisses or quick pecks.

As disappointed as Stephanie was that it was ending, this would go down as one of the best acted and least likely to be doubted as real relationships she had participated in scripting. The tabloids were all speculating loudly about their relationship and Devon's show had never been so popular.

Sadly, Nora had been keeping herself scarce, just a quick check-in or friendly text now and then, not wanting to cause any more drama between the couple than was already there. Stephanie really wanted to tell her the truth, but it just impossible right now. Guilt ate at her more than she'd care to admit. The first potential female friend in years and she was deceiving her.

At least the media had been leaving Nora out of their relationship drama. For now, anyway.

Stephanie pulled out the biggest guns she owned for the event. After stepping into her black lace Manolo Blahnik heels, she adjusted her invisible bra—which was basically a couple of pieces of miracle tape holding her breasts in place—and wondered for the millionth time if it was really the best idea to wear the Stella McCartney lace peek-a-boo gown. It was jaw-droppingly gorgeous and she never got a chance to wear it. It had potential wardrobe malfunction written all over it with eight inches of lace down both sides eliminating any possibility of underthings for the woman who put it on.

"Screw it." She sighed and threw her shoulders back. To hell with anyone who thought her fit frame was too big for leading-lady acting. Stephanie decided that she was going to rock that dress.

She chose simple garnet jewelry to accessorize, and a black clutch to hold her lipstick, keys, and phone. The gate buzzed as she hurried to get her earrings on.

For this event, Devon had been supplied a limo by the studio. It was a blockbuster movie premiere, after all, and they had to show up in style.

Stephanie buzzed open the gate after confirming it was really the car Devon had sent and was nearly to the front door when the bell rang.

"Holy…wow." Devon gaped at her as he took in the dress. His eyes traveled in a slow heated sweep from her hair to her shoes. He took a step back as though the full impact of her had physically knocked him back a pace.

Stephanie felt the blush crawl up her neck and face, hot and fast, suddenly nervous.

"Too much?"

He shook his head. "No. Not at all. You look stunning. I can't even find the right words to say it properly."

Stephanie laughed, feeling the nervous blush shift from her face to an area of her body much more centralized and currently without even a scrap of cloth over it.

"You clean up pretty well yourself, Mr. Greene. Nice suit."

He smiled and pretended to adjust his powder blue silk tie, the driver holding open the door and tipping his hat to her as they climbed into the back of the stretch.

"Armani?" Stephanie asked, carefully adjusting herself and the gown on the leather seat.

"Naturally. Best piece of clothing I own."

"I can relate."

He gazed at her approvingly.

"Honestly, Stephanie, you look ridiculously incredible."

"Thank you." She could feel herself blushing a bit. "So. Are we going to enjoy the movie, or not?"

Devon grinned. "Yes. I figured red carpet with tense faces and fake smiles, some whispered bickering in the theater and then the big drama on the carpet on the way out."

Stephanie nodded. "That's what I was thinking. Besides, I really want to see the movie."

Devon laughed. "Me too. Been looking forward to it for weeks."

All too soon they were pulling into the queue of cars in front of Mann's Chinese theater. There was the expected gaggle of paparazzi and camera crews and entertainment reporters getting sound bites.

"Here we go." Devon sighed, squeezing her hand briefly before she slid as carefully out of the car as she had into it.

Stephanie and Devon waved, fake smiled and put on their tense faces while they posed. Devon gave thoughtful answers to inane questions as reporters approached them. Stephanie focused on making it look as though her smile was pasted on—which considering the blinding nature of all the camera flashes wasn't all that difficult—and tried to not be insulted when on the rare occasion the reporter asked her a question it was usually about her mother or Devon instead of her—or they asked about her sex life.

As they made their way down the maze of cameras, Stephanie had a fleeting thought that it was like shopping at Ikea. A giant rat trap designed for one entrance and one exit and you had to look at every single thing in the store before being allowed to leave. She very nearly giggled but covered it with a cough.

Devon took that opportunity to glare at her, then faked a grin for the cameras. She followed his lead and rolled her eyes, looking disinterested and barely managing a grin for the last bit of picture taking.

As they were ushered inside the lobby of the theater, Devon put on a cross face but whispered in her ear proudly. "Well done. They ate that up like candy."

She shot him a withering look, instead of the smile she wanted to give, a glare which she saw was noticed by no fewer than two dozen people milling about the theater lobby.

Finally, they were allowed to take their seats. The movie started and a few minutes in, Stephanie harshly whispered something to Devon about the soda he had purchased not being diet.

"Get your own then. Jesus." He replied.

Stephanie put on an incredulous face and crossed her arms over her chest.

A while later, when Devon made a move to put his arm around her shoulders, she shrugged him off quite forcefully.

What seemed like halfway through the movie—which they were both genuinely enjoying—Stephanie barked in a loud whisper, "What do you mean you didn't get me any candy?"

They kept finding small things to pretend snipe at one another about until the movie was over—not enough napkins for the popcorn, too much extra butter, no chocolate-covered peanuts, too much ice in the non-diet soda, it was an endless list and wholly entertaining. They were shushed and glared at and ended up being 'those people' much to their own, well-disguised amusement. As the house lights came up and the theater emptied, they sat in stony silence, both looking pissed and uncomfortable. Everyone around them noticed.

Stephanie couldn't help but be pleased and it took an effort not to show it. Their ruse was working, and she was proud of them for pulling it off in such spectacular fashion.

As they filed back through the lobby heading toward the exit doors where a bit of organized chaos queued all the celebrities up for their limousines, Devon gave her a slight nod.

"Just *STOP*, Stephanie, Jesus. I work with her, okay? It's not like I can just never see her again. She happens to be my friend." He whispered this harshly, quiet but loudly enough that the lobby grew quiet and turned to watch once they discovered there was something dramatic happening.

Stephanie glared at him, and to his credit, he didn't waver, blue eyes blazing, face set in a jaw-clenching expression of anger.

"You bastard." Stephanie began to shake a bit, nerves and excitement compounding in the adrenaline running through her veins. "I *knew* it. She tried to snake her way into being my friend too." She could feel the hundreds of eyes turned their way. A low buzz ran through the crowd and the heat of a thousand flashbulbs pushed her forward.

She instantly regretted this tactic. Nora was not at fault here, and now it looked like Stephanie believed something about her she knew not to be true.

"*I knew it!*" Stephanie's heart and mind were in conflict. She knew it was fake but it felt real and it echoed some things in her past too perfectly for her not to have a real reaction. She hoped she could separate the two out later. Right now, it made good theater. They would owe Nora all the apologies for this.

"Oh, come on." He sniped back at her. "She's my *friend*, I'm not sleeping with her or anything. Not that I've been sleeping with *you*, either." He glared at her, then mumbled, "Let's just say the word frigid doesn't even begin to cover it." Several people gasped.

Stephanie closed the small distance between them with a firmly planted Manolo and slapped his cheek with her open hand, the satisfying crack resounding through the open room. She could hear several exclamations and the frantic click of camera lenses.

"We're *done*." Stephanie growled. As he cradled his cheek in one hand, she turned on her heel and stormed out of the theater, heads swiveling as they watched her leave and then snapped back to see Devon's reaction.

She could hear him grouse as casually as he could, "Women. Am I right?" To which there were several responding grunts of assent.

The cool evening embraced Stephanie as the doors of the theater closed behind her. Luckily a fleet of vehicles was standing by because of the event and in no time, she was safely inside a taxi, an unusual occurrence in Los Angeles. She gave her parents' address and prayed the cabbie either didn't recognize her or at least was one that didn't make a big deal over it. It crossed her mind that the dress she was wearing certainly didn't help her be forgettable.

The city flew by her window in a flash of lights and storefronts, and despite the pull of her heart indicating that she was sad to be done with Devon, she was smiling. That had been a fantastically fun way to end a job.

She had the cabbie drop her at the curb and waited for him to pull away before keying in her gate code. It was a long walk up the driveway, but the night was balmy and mild and she felt like walking off the remnants of her adrenaline from the theater break up performance was a good idea.

As she was slipping out of the fantastic dress and carefully storing the Manolos back in their box, her cell phone chimed at her. Picking it up off of the bedspread, she couldn't help but smile.

D: *That was great. Thanks for everything. See you soon?*

Stephanie thought for a moment about how to respond. For this to work, unless they wanted to start rumors of getting back together, they wouldn't be seeing each other around town. At least not on purpose. Or on friendly terms.

S: *Maybe. Glad I could help you out.*

That seemed really blasé and generic, but she wasn't sure exactly what she was supposed to say.

In a couple of weeks, when the dust settled, she'd reach out to Nora. Despite the drive to do so right away, things had to settle down and the gossip factories had to move on to another target first.

Stephanie made an attempt at taking a relaxing bath and then camped out on the sofa, watching John Hughes movies until the wee hours of the morning.

CHAPTER
Eleven

STEPHANIE WAS DISORIENTED for a few days with no dates to plan out and no place to be after weeks of a pretty regular out and about schedule.

She made the mistake of turning on one of the tabloid news shows and got to see herself slap Devon in slow motion, on repeat, and over again and listen to the so-called reporters speculate about whether or not it was really over and if he had in fact moved on to dating his co-star.

Stephanie's eyebrow raised at that suggestion, though she knew it was Devon himself who planted it with the media. It was an interesting idea, but she knew the slender blonde named Nora Chase was not Devon's love interest. Not really. They were platonic friends, and for a moment, Nora had been her friend too.

Feeling a moment of jealousy about it infuriated Stephanie. It was most certainly a holdover from what had happened with her former friends and her ex.

"He was a client, you weirdo. Knock it off." But he had also been what felt like a good friend for nearly two months. Stephanie was having a hard time reconciling the gap in her mind.

It was Marty's phone call that broke her out of her aimless daze.

"Kid! That was spectacular! Great slap, by the way. I think they heard that out in Pasadena."

Stephanie laughed. "Thanks, Marty. As far as fake break-ups go, that was a fun one."

Marty chuckled. "Look, I don't want to spring this on you so soon, but we've had an offer I think we need to consider."

Stephanie made her way into the office and sat down in the leather chair at her desk. She watched the birds play in the big stone birdbath outside the window while she waited for the computer to boot up.

"That much money being thrown around, huh?"

Marty laughed, but she knew she had nailed the reason. "You got it, kid. Two million—upfront—for thirty days."

Stephanie felt her eyes go wide and sat up straight in her chair.

"What? That's crazy. Who is it?"

"Here's where I ask you to consider it, even though you're not going to like it."

Inwardly, Stephanie groaned. "You've never steered me wrong, Marty, but you're making me nervous right now. Who?"

Marty heaved a sigh. "Brett Masterson."

Stephanie just stared at the birds. Brett Masterson had just been released from the county jail after serving an extremely truncated sentence for attempted manslaughter. He had been accused of hit and run. The pedestrian victim may or may not have been his lover.

Something about the case had never felt quite right to Stephanie. There were too many convenient or missing pieces when it came right down to it. The reports had left out huge potholes of information. Some reports claimed he wasn't even in the city at the time the accident occurred. For some reason, his team seemed to only fight the accusation half-heartedly and he had appeared none too bothered to have to serve a few weeks in jail over the ordeal.

Maybe it was her heightened lie sensor from being the Image Adjuster, but something smelled completely fishy about the whole situation. She couldn't help but wonder if there was some kind of weird payoff involved, or if the whole thing had been a bizarre publicity stunt.

"You can't be serious, Marty. Do you know something I don't? That case is definitely strange."

She could hear the tension in Marty's voice. "Thirty days, Kid. That's maybe a dozen dates if you're overachieving, maybe only four if your magic works as fast as I think it will." He paused, waiting for her reaction.

Stephanie pinched the bridge of her nose with her fingertips.

She'd put a decent amount of money down that Marty had plenty of information about Brett Masterson that he would never in this lifetime share with her or anybody else. He would never endanger her though, that much was certain. Part of her brain couldn't believe she was considering this. The other part operated her mouth without her control.

"Thirty days. I'll agree to a maximum of eight public appearances. That's two a week. Make sure you inform his people of all the fine details of our contracts. If he is inappropriate or untoward in any way, shape or form, we're done and they forfeit the fee." She swallowed, pushing forward. "Even if it's in the first ten minutes of our first date—if he is anything less than gentlemanly or charming, we're done and I still get paid. The full fee."

She felt dirty. It was never about money for her. Never. What was she doing?

Marty chuckled, it was a knowing and proud sound from deep in his throat. "I'll draw the docs up. You're a tough cookie, Kid. I'm honored to work with you."

Stephanie relaxed her shoulders and managed a feeble smile. "Learned from the best, Marty. I'll watch for the paperwork."

"You got it. Take care, Kid."

Stephanie hung up the phone and had a moment of panic. What in the world had she just agreed to? Why was she even considering another contract, especially one like this right now? She reached for the phone more than once, but in the end, her need to stick to her commitments won out. She'd said yes, so she was locked in as far as her brain was concerned.

And her brain was a total traitor. Why had she said yes?

Rather than sit around and think about it, she tried to spend some time painting. The application of paint on canvas was as discombobulated and messy as her emotional state was. Her thoughts were disorderly and so was her creativity—and not in a good way. Mostly she felt like she was just pretending to create anything, but thankfully a call from Maxwell saved her from further artistic fraud.

His name flashed across her screen and she couldn't suppress the smile. Hastily wiping her paint dappled hands on a towel, she swiped to accept his call and put him on speaker.

"To what do I owe this honor? I already spoke with our 'uncle' Marty today. I expect to talk to your father rather soon too."

"My deepest apologies and heartfelt sympathies."

"No need. Marty was making me a rather obscenely priced business proposition."

"Well, then I take it back."

Stephanie smiled. Maxwell's native language was money. Hers was not. Hers was…coming up blank, she frowned again.

"How are you, Maxwell?"

He laughed. "You're doing this wrong, Alex. That's my line."

Stephanie let out a breath and picked up the phone, pressing it to her ear instead of leaving it on speaker. "I'm fine, Max. Why wouldn't I be?"

"Come on, Alex. This is *me* you're talking to. You just had a very public, very ugly break up and he is being accused of cheating on you. And by the sounds of it, you're going to rebound straight into another pretend relationship. I want to know how you're doing. Really."

"And you already know that what was going on there was not all that it seemed, Max." Even her supposedly secure cellphone seemed a dangerous place to spill any kind of beans about their relationship having been fake.

"I know you, Alex. I see you. And I know that he was really into you. I think you might have felt the same, even if you didn't want to. I'm sorry."

Stephanie stared off into space as the blast of hurt unraveled in her chest and slowly moved through her body. It would seem she was prepared for anything but genuine sympathy. "Thanks."

He sighed. "Does this call for Mr. Woo's?"

Stephanie found herself laughing, but there were tears in her eyes.

"Nah. Maybe steak though. And crab. Maybe a disgustingly large slice of chocolate cake."

"Oh, my darling Alex, you know just how to talk dirty to me."

And just like that, Stephanie had a dinner date with her best and oldest friend, a reason to shower and dress, and no further expectations.

CHAPTER
Twelve

SOONER THAN SHE was prepared for, Stephanie was meeting Brett Masterson at an out of the way gourmet hamburger restaurant for their first date. She couldn't remember having been this nervous in a long time, not even on her last real first date which had been, well, too long ago to recall, actually.

She'd even had to give herself a pep-talk both before leaving the house and in the car. Floundering was probably an appropriate word for what she was doing since her fake split from Devon, a client.

It didn't make any sense to feel so out of sorts, but she was not in a very good place. Certainly part of it was the loss of the friendship, but she'd never felt so adrift after losing a friend or finishing a job before. In this case, she'd lost both Devon and Nora—perhaps that was the difference. Before, with her ex and former friends, they had all done something she considered unforgivable. The loss of them hurt but was better than the damage they'd already done.

This new floaty experience was disconcerting and she was tired of feeling like she was existing only partially in her own body.

Even though this new contract was really unorthodox for her, she hoped it would help snap her out of her post-Devon Greene malaise.

He saw her walk in and waved her over to a booth. He was ruggedly handsome, very tall and had an edge of danger to him. Stephanie imagined that all those things combined actually usually worked in his favor most of the time. He had dark blonde hair and hazel eyes.

Brett forced a grin as she approached the table.

"Hi." He muttered.

"Hi, Brett." Stephanie put on her best comfortable-and-happy-to-be-here smile. "So nice of Sandra to set us up." She spoke in code, referring to his publicist and all the instructions Stephanie had passed along to make this as painless a process as possible.

"Yes, it is." He nodded.

Stephanie began to worry a bit about how any conversation was going to go.

"Great." She flashed him a thousand-watt smile that she didn't really feel, hoping it would ease some of the tension between them.

It seemed to work, though only a tiny bit.

"Sandra said these aren't real dates." His eyes were somehow very childlike and darted around the nearly empty restaurant, voice almost a whisper.

Stephanie nodded and lowered her voice to almost match his as they began to look over the menus. She glanced up as Alan casually strolled into the restaurant and took a seat at the counter. She relaxed a bit. He wouldn't let anything happen to her on his watch.

"That's right. I mean, they are real in the sense that we actually go out and do things and are seen together. They aren't real in that I'm an actress, pretending to be dating you so that you can get your career back on track. When we go our separate ways for the day, I don't expect you to call me, or text. You are free to do whatever you need to do. The paperwork outlines the specifics of what's on the table and expected as far as things like physical contact."

Brett visibly relaxed. "Okay. I think I get it now." He gave her a somewhat sheepish smile.

Stephanie wondered how someone like him had survived jail time. Despite his size, he seemed like a shy, almost meek guy. His size was imposing, he had to be at least six foot three and two hundred fifty pounds, but he seemed like a giant squish ball.

This might not be so bad after all.

They ordered their burgers and Stephanie gave him some gentle coaching on body language, talking him through the things she was doing so he understood why she was moving how she was, the expressions on her face and how he could help her do her job well by participating.

By the time the check came, Stephanie was anticipating that this contract would be a somewhat easy ride for 30 days and a big fat paycheck.

A big part of her despised that she thought that way. The money was never the first thing she considered when taking a contract. She liked the thrill of winning by turning around a client's image. She loved being able to practice the craft of acting in a meaningful way. The fact that money was what she was focusing on further convinced her that she was in a very strange mental space and that she needed to find a way out of it, fast.

She left Brett in front of the restaurant and after a quick, covert conversation and hug with Alan, who she realized she had heartily missed, she headed to the grocery store for a few odds and ends, then back to her parents' house where she cleaned up her email boxes, sent a long missive to her parents who were now wrapping up a long journey through the United Kingdom and a quick message to Marty to let him know that the first date had gone well with Brett.

The next few days were spent painting and relaxing. There was a pretty smooth dinner date with Brett at Boa Steakhouse, where the paparazzi got plenty of photographic evidence they were there out together. Brett wasn't much of a conversationalist, but once Stephanie figured out he was interested in cars, his tongue seemed to loosen up and they had a pretty decent meal. She knew enough to keep asking questions and he had plenty of enthusiasm to keep talking.

TMZ and other sites were all abuzz with the news of their date the following day, and already the tide was turning for Brett. Many were discussing how the evidence against him had seemed planted or circumstantial, and others were lauding that he was somehow the better man for just doing the time without trying to use his celebrity or image as leverage to get himself a lighter sentence, better treatment or anything of the like. There was discussion about everything Stephanie wondered about as well— whether or not the situation had gone down as reported and why there seemed to be so many holes in the story.

All in all, it was positive spin for the quiet giant, and she was pleased things were going well with the media.

After their dinner date, Stephanie arranged a movie and coffee for the next week, and both seemed to go smoothly. Brett was warming up to her and she was getting a good acting muscle workout trying to pretend she was super into him. He seemed like a nice guy, was certainly handsome, but he just wasn't great company most of the time.

Brett was for sure the strong, silent type; and while that was totally understandable and likely just a personality trait, it was making Stephanie's job quite complicated.

She now understood why the offered fee was so high. She was definitely working for her paycheck, but she didn't feel uncomfortable like she had expected which was nice.

As a bonus, she was getting to see Alan every time she went out with Brett, if only from across a restaurant.

As the third week of Brett dates approached, Stephanie heaved a sigh of relief that they had made it past the halfway point and that the job would be over soon. She found it relatively amusing that she had been concerned initially that Brett was a danger to her, violent in any way or used to throwing around his muscle to intimidate. The exact opposite was true—he was a shy, quiet guy who had to be steered through basic conversation. Stephanie was getting bored holding up entire dates by herself.

One evening as she was flipping through TV channels, eating Ben and Jerry's ice cream straight out of the pint with a spoon, she saw that Devon was reported to be dating Nora. The tabloids were all over the beautiful couple as they were spotted coming out of his place for a morning run and coffee stop before heading to the set. The so-called journalists were discussing how Nora had been there as support after the ugly breakup between Devon and Stephanie, and likely it had brought the two closer than their previous friendship had been.

Stephanie shook her head, trying to ignore the burn she felt under her ribcage. Nora wasn't right for Devon, and they were platonic friends, just like she and Maxwell, right? What if that hadn't been completely true after all? Nora had reached out a few times, but not much at all since the breakup. There had never seemed a good time or good way to explain what had happened without orchestrating a conversation involving Devon and that hadn't been possible.

Stephanie still lamented that the budding friendship between herself and Nora had fizzled before it really even had a chance to get started.

Devon and Stephanie had seemed to have a decent friendship, but he had been paying her for a service, after all, and they hadn't spoken a word since the text following their breakup, so who knew what was real anymore.

"Don't let her break your heart." Stephanie found herself mumbling, looking into Devon's crystal blue eyes through the LED television screen. It wasn't wrong for her to care about what happened to him; Stephanie just wished she didn't care quite so much.

AFTER ANOTHER FANCY dinner and bowling, of all things, Stephanie was counting down the days to her and Brett parting ways. Without any prompting from her or any knowledge, as a matter of fact, he had already been spotted out and about with another young starlet, one that seemed much better suited to him.

Catherine Johannes was a knockout former model with legs that were at least six feet long and bright red hair. She was a firecracker to Brett's introvert.

The gossip sites were all abuzz with the news and

Stephanie was not altogether surprised to get a phone call as the final week started.

"Contract has been fulfilled, you are hereby released from any future engagements with Mr. Brett Masterson."

Stephanie flopped onto the couch and sighed. "Thank you, Marty. Best news I've had all day."

"Glad to be of service, kid. Wasn't all that bad for that kind of dough, huh?"

"Not at all. He's a sweet guy, just not my speed. He'll be okay with Catherine, I think. She'll take care of him. Did we do what we set out to from the PR standpoint?"

Marty laughed a throaty guffaw. "You bet. People were terrified of him before, scared he would fly off the handle and hurt someone again—if, in fact, he hurt anyone to begin with. Now they are questioning everything about the hit and run case and offering him work. You did good, kid, very good, without even trying."

"Thanks, Marty." She thought for a moment. "No more contracts for a while, okay? I'm going to take some time."

"Sure thing. You deserve it." Marty shuffled some paperwork around. "Hear from your folks?"

Stephanie laughed. "Funny you should ask. Mom called just yesterday and they are finally headed home for a while. They should be here day after tomorrow."

"That's fantastic! Have your dad give me a call, okay? I want to see the family and have dinner."

"You got it, Marty. Thanks again. I appreciate it."

"My pleasure, kid. Talk to you soon."

Stephanie hung up the phone, feeling light and unanchored in her own body. With a quick change into a new pin-up model inspired suit, she headed out to the pool to swim away any lingering worries and soak up some much-needed sunshine.

Chapter Thirteen

STEPHANIE ARRANGED FOR Mary, the family's housekeeper, to give the house a thorough shine before Marlowe and Peter arrived back home. Mary gushed about how glad she was to be getting back to her regular schedule.

"I love my kids and I adore my grandbabies, but I have been missing my other family." Mary gave Stephanie a hug before getting ready to leave for the day, the house aglow and smelling of fresh linens and lemon in her wake.

"You know we love you, Mary. You're family to us too."

Stephanie wasn't exaggerating. Mary had always been a part of the household and her life and she missed her when she was away. It had never hurt that Mary was the best cook anyone knew and baked the best cakes in the entire world. Stephanie suspected that Mary had been concerned about the drop-in hours in regard to her bank account. Unbeknownst to her, Marlowe had prepared for such a thing and hadn't adjusted her pay one bit despite the vacation. Family was family, and Mary certainly deserved it for her devotion to the Von Feldts.

Around lunchtime the following day, Marlowe and Peter arrived by town car, and it took nearly thirty minutes to get all the luggage unloaded and inside the house.

Marlowe swept Stephanie up in a warm soft hug, the familiar scent of roses and oranges making her smile.

"Oh, darling! We missed you!" Marlowe held Stephanie at arm's length, giving her a good looking at. Stephanie had put on the Caroline Herrera dress to be sure she was dressed appropriately for her mom. "You look so wonderful! Have you kept busy while we were away? Thank you so much for keeping an eye on the house. I know you have been enjoying your independence." Marlowe swooped down and planted a loud, lipsticky kiss on Stephanie's cheek before Peter took his daughter into a firm embrace.

"Hi, honey." He smiled broadly at her, the grey hair at his temples giving him a distinguished air.

"Hi, Dad." Stephanie smiled, and he kissed her forehead. She was mush in his arms, musing that there was nothing quite like the love between and father and daughter.

As the group adjourned to the living room to unpack the bevy of gifts and trinkets they had picked up on their travels, Stephanie gave them the short version of what she had been up to while they were gone.

"Marty found me a couple of clients, so I have been working. The last one was a whale though, so I'm going to take some time off, maybe focus on my painting for a while." She beamed as her mother pulled a Parisian silk scarf around Stephanie's neck, then produced a number of pieces of jewelry, some pottery from Spain and coins from all over the world, both new and ancient.

"That's good, dear. You're so talented. I'm glad Marty kept you busy." Her father grinned at her, watching his wife bury their daughter in gifts.

"Will you be going back to your apartment then?" Marlowe looked a bit disappointed.

"Not for a couple of days. I figured I would help you get unpacked and hear all about your travels before I go."

Marlowe clapped her impeccably manicured hands. "Oh good. I must tell you about the food! Oh, just so delicious and decadent everywhere we went! The architecture in Spain is simply a sight, Stephanie, truly. And the shopping! Oh, the shopping!"

"I can see the shopping was pretty great, Mom." Stephanie laughed.

Marlowe went on and on, Stephanie eventually plunking herself down on the couch next to her father who slid an arm around her shoulders. Marlowe enthusiastically told all about the places they had seen, the shops she had visited and the items she just had to bring home.

"There will likely be some deliveries in the next few days."

"There's more?" Stephanie asked, incredulous. Where would they put it all?

"Naturally, dear. It's not every day you take a three-month journey across the continent, is it? Anyway, then there was the Black Forest. I have never seen such a wonderful area! The trees and wildlife, simply unbelievable…"

As Marlowe droned on, Stephanie allowed her mind to wander, interested smile plastered on her face. She loved her mother, she really, really did. However, she was certain that after two or three days of this kind of thing she would be more than ready for the peace and quiet of her beachside apartment.

TRUE TO HER word, Stephanie left her parents' house with only a fraction of the gifts they had brought her back from Europe three days later. She drove away from the house, waving broadly as her parents watched from the front steps, in her metallic blue Mini Cooper convertible. She had gotten used to being up off the ground in her father's Land Rover but was happy to feel like she was in her car, heading towards her home.

Usually, she would have taken the more scenic route along the pacific coast highway after traveling through Topanga Canyon, but today she didn't want to waste the extra 45 minutes to go the long way around. Stephanie steered her little car onto highway 101 and drove like the devil was chasing her out of L.A.

Santa Barbara was less than two hours from Los Angeles, but to Stephanie, it was a comfortable world away.

She parked her car in the small covered garage behind the building and used her key to enter the cool concrete hallway between the restaurant her loft was above, and the trendy beachwear shop next door. She walked almost to the entrance door at the front of the building, driven to go straight to the beach, but turned and went up the steps instead. At the landing, she turned left.

She had bought a similar apartment on the right side of the landing above the clothing store, but she wasn't quite finished renovating it.

She had been teasing Maxwell about buying it for himself, and soon. He turned her down at every offering, but she knew he was considering it from the look he got in his eyes. That would make for an interesting neighbor situation, but a welcome one.

She just hoped he decided one way or the other before she started picking out the final finishes. Maybe she'd decorate for Maxwell's taste regardless, simplify things. Surely if he passed, a slightly more masculine but beachy palate would appeal to another buyer.

Stephanie sat down the bags of trinkets she had carried from the car and slid her key into the lock, the breath that left her when she opened the door a very cleansing sigh of homecoming.

The loft was one giant open space, full of light and air and warmth.

Stephanie had chosen many of the details herself, and the huge skylights were one of her favorite things. Floor to ceiling windows allowed her to see out either end of the loft, and the skylights illuminated the rest of the open brick-walled space.

The building the loft was in had been built in the early 1900s as a general mercantile store. The upstairs had been all storage in those days, but Stephanie had immediately seen the potential for living space when she had been shown the dirty, run-down place a year before. The original brickwork was left exposed, reclaimed lumber used for flooring. She had spared no expense to restore as many original details as she could while putting in place all the modern conveniences she could ever want.

To the right of the door was an open living room space with three plush micro suede couches in a silvery blue color forming a horseshoe around a barn-wood coffee table. On the wall was a flat panel TV that Stephanie seldom watched, and a nearly flat gas fireplace.

Against the bank of windows at the back of the building was the open kitchen with recycled glass countertops, frosted glass-fronted cabinetry and stainless appliances, all shining and clean lines. There was a dining area along the windows as well, a long farmhouse table and benches lit by a rustic wrought iron chandelier. Marlowe had doubted the casual mixing of the rustic and ultra-modern styles, but it worked well and Stephanie absolutely loved it.

All along the wall opposite the door were canvases. The completed works were all hung, the in-progress ones stacked sometimes five deep along the floor. They were all different sizes and stages, and four easels stood at different vantage points along the long wall for different angles of lighting. Stephanie had asked that three shelving units be built out of steel and glass for her painting supplies. The cabinets stood at the far end of the wall, near the front bank of windows, and matched the kitchen cabinetry. One extra-large set at the very end concealed a sleek washer and dryer unit.

At the front of the building was an open bedroom, blocked off only by a few well-placed antique panel screens. The bank of floor to ceiling windows looked out on the curve of beach and ocean that was less than a block's walk away. Stephanie had found a local craftsman to make her a four-poster bed and closet units out of natural lumber, and he had supplied exactly what she wanted, the bed looking twisted and bent and wholly of the earth, the closet units making it feel almost as though she had a couple of trees in her room. She had draped gauzy fabric around the posts to give a softer, more princess feel, and put down a plush sheepskin like rug underneath to treat her feet to some decadence when she got out of bed.

The front corner of the room, exactly the other end from the kitchen was a lavish but compact bathroom. There was an eight-head steam shower and jetted tub, every luxury a girl could want.

Stephanie hauled the bags inside and closed the door behind herself.

She opened the fridge to find nothing but a box of baking soda, a half-empty jar of green olives and some bottles of water. For a moment Stephanie just wandered around her space, reacquainting herself with it.

Her fingertips skimmed the countertops and the shiny smooth surface of the farmhouse table. Her eyes assessed a few of the unfinished canvasses and she let her mind wander as to what she wanted to do to complete them. She took a moment to freshen up in the bathroom, combing out and re-tying her unruly chocolate hair into a knot on top of her head and changing into a gauzy summer dress and sandals that were a staple for her time at the beach.

Unable to commit to anything, she wandered down the stairs to the restaurant and pub and decided that a beer on the patio would do her soul and indecisive mind good.

It was three beers and some fish tacos from a street cart later that she finally motivated to walk a few blocks over to the grocery store, and another beer on the way back before she finally went back up to her loft, feeling wholly relaxed and at peace and where she belonged.

CHAPTER Fourteen

STEPHANIE PAINTED LIKE mad, all hours of the day and night for weeks. It was as though being in Hollywood had sparked a frenzy of need for her artistic side. She had brought two of the larger canvases she had finished while at her parents' house with her, and they hung on either side of the television in the living room.

As a counter to the two smaller canvases, above the television, was a series of three large ones. Each was an abstract representation of a different flower. There was a calla lily, a hydrangea, and a day lily—Stephanie's favorite blooms. The canvases were the work of Stephanie's grandmother, Marlena—Marlowe's mother.

She could vividly remember sitting down at the worn white and gold-flecked Formica breakfast bar with her Granny, finger paints and butcher paper laid out for her. Later, it was cheap watercolors and thick construction paper. Eventually, Granny Marlena graduated her to an actual easel, canvases and real paints, teaching her the ins and outs of how to move the brush, dab the paint, smudge the shading. Stephanie smiled, thinking of Granny Lena. She had been gone a number of years, but Stephanie had nearly all of her artwork, so she was never far away.

Most of Stephanie's meals were being supplied by the Irish pub and grill downstairs, but she did manage to get down to the ocean for some good laps most days. Once the painting frenzy burned itself out, she found herself spending more and more time on the beach, and she even went so far as to reserve a cabana—which was really just a bit of all-weather tent fabric draped on posts covering two lounge chairs and a table on three sides and a roof—for the remainder of the Summer.

Stephanie's routine quickly became rising late in the morning, grabbing a sandwich from the deli down the street on her way to the beach, going down to the cabana and reading a book for about an hour, taking a swim, reading a bit more of the book, returning home to shower, eat something from the pub downstairs and paint into the wee hours of the morning.

The constant splatter of paint on her forearm and hands ceased to bother her, it became standard to see her in one of the gauzy sundresses, or a cotton maxi-dress and sandals over a bathing suit. Her hair was constantly unruly with natural curl or pinned up in a loose gather-ing on top of her head. The tan on her skin grew deeper and laps in the pull of the ocean further tightened her muscular physique.

Liam, the manager of the Irish pub, O'Malley's, and the staff both there and at the deli were really the only people she spoke to with any regularity. She, of course, communicated often with her parents but didn't often venture home to visit. They had a monthly date where they met in Malibu or Topanga for lunch, but that was really it. She and Maxwell similarly tried to meet up somewhere every few weeks in addition to talking more regularly on the phone. Marlowe and Maxwell seemed worried, but Stephanie assured them that she was just figuring some things out.

She didn't feel like she was though. There was still an odd floating to her life since the contract with Devon had ended. She lacked direction. While not overly bothersome, the sensation of falling or spinning out of control would sneak up on her now and then, demanding she formulate a plan. Inevitably, Stephanie would bat it away and continue on as though painting and swimming and isolating herself was the plan. Deep down, she knew it wasn't, but she hadn't yet figured out what direction she needed to go.

Stephanie had sold a number of the finished paintings since returning to her loft, which somehow bolstered her need to paint even more—which at the very least was motivation and a possible direction.

One very large abstract in shades of azure and mint with a touch of tangerine in the background had gone to the Beverly Wilshire lobby. A set of three floral-inspired abstracts (an homage to Granny Lena's trio) had been snapped up by a buyer for one of Wolfgang Puck's restaurants and were adorning the wall behind the host stand at Hotel Bel Air. Several stand-alone smaller paintings had been sold to buyers throughout Southern California.

Stephanie wasn't sure whether her parents or Marty was promoting her so well, but it was a wonderful feeling that so many appreciated the labor of her soul.

Marty had attempted to talk her into a couple more contracts, but Stephanie wasn't interested.

"I need a long break, Marty. I appreciate that there's interest, I'm just feeling a little burned out." She looked out the window at the ocean, watching the relaxing roll of waves. "Besides, I'm having too much success painting to put that on hold right now. I'm happy hiding out in Santa Barbara for the moment."

Marty laughed.

"I can't hold that against you, kid. You're doing great. Find yourself. I wish I had known who I was at your age."

Stephanie laughed. "Shouldn't I have figured it out by now? My clock is ticking by Hollywood standards. 27 is positively old."

Marty guffawed and she fondly pictured his slightly off-kilter glasses and tie.

"You said it, not me, darling. Things are different now. Take your time. Do what you love. Not many have that luxury. Enjoy it. Call Maxwell, would you? I think he's going through something and he's not about to confide in his old man or me—I'm just the crazy, nosy uncle."

Stephanie thanked him, promising she would call Max (she had also noticed that something was definitely up with him) and at the very least that she would come home for Thanksgiving as that was her mother's favorite holiday and there was always a three-day party for all of the friends and family through their home to celebrate.

"Just need some time." She mumbled to herself, still watching the waves. Stephanie felt oddly disconnected from everything but her painting. Some time was what she needed, but there's no way she could have predicted that her respite would be so short.

STEPHANIE HAD JUST retrieved her daily sandwich—turkey on rye with extra veggies—and a large bottle of water from the deli and was digging around in her huge straw beach bag for her sunglasses as she wandered down the sidewalk toward the beach.

Someone bumped into her at full force on her right side.

Before she could stop it, her oversized bag jolted from her arm and the bottle of water flew from her hand and began to roll away.

"Sorry! I'll get it!" The man she had run into dashed aside to grab the bottle as Stephanie gathered the other items that had scattered from her bag.

Stephanie stood up and accepted the bottle from the man's hand.

"Thanks." She gave an apologetic smile and found herself stunned into silence.

The man standing in front of her in a very comfortable pair of white linen pants, beach sandals and a barely-buttoned blue linen shirt the exact color of his eyes was none other than Devon Greene. The fedora hat he was wearing matched the pants perfectly. It was also a fantastic sunblock and face shield if he looked down.

"I'm so sorry, I'm such a klutz." He gaped at her, then made no attempt to hide the heated up and down sweep of her he did with his eyes. "Stephanie?"

"Devon!" Stephanie very nearly squeaked, heart pounding. "Hi! How are you?"

"I'm great, but you! You're *fantastic*." He was unabashedly taking her in. "I mean really. You look positively incredible."

Without hesitation, he drew her in for a quick hug. It was just a moment, but it loosened that hinge in her chest again, the one that had started to tighten down again. She could feel it, and she was as grateful as she was nervous.

Stephanie took a moment to wonder if he was putting her on, but nobody was that good. She blushed.

"Thanks, you're no slouch yourself. Beach linen suits you."

He gave that devastating grin and she began to fidget with her bag. The nerves she'd only ever felt around him were back, and in full force.

"What, ah, brings you to the beach?" Stephanie asked, gesturing to the sand and waves about a half a block from them.

"I needed some time away. The show is done for the season, I was sick of the city. And I can only spend so much time back home with the family."

Stephanie nodded and they had an unusual awkward moment of silence as Stephanie tried to calculate the odds of him showing up in this exact spot.

"How's Nora?" She asked, putting on her most polite curious smile.

Devon looked at his hands, then back at Stephanie.

"Ah. You haven't heard? That was a very short-lived rumor. I feel like you should definitely know that it was never anything more than a rumor. Nora and I…"

"Are like me and Maxwell." Stephanie supplied, seeing his intense discomfort. Her heart kicked into high gear and her hopes shot way up into the stratosphere.

"Precisely. By the time you were wrapping things up with Brett Masterson—which, really? Brett Masterson? We have to talk about that—the press had lost their interest because there was clearly nothing but friendship going on there." He gave a shrug. "Like I said when we first met, relationships, even pretend ones I guess, have never been my strong suit."

Stephanie nodded. "I'm sorry the press latched on to that. I like her. We were friends, or something like it, for a short while."

"She's still your friend, Steph. So am I. I explained what I could to her, which honestly wasn't much and we don't keep secrets. All you gotta do is reach out." That boyish grin and piercing eyes very nearly undid Stephanie right there on the sidewalk.

"As you say, then." A million questions swirled in her mind, but she forced them down. Stephanie glanced around. "What were your plans for the day? I can make some recommendations."

He shrugged and looked around. "I have been window shopping this morning. Considered the beach." He shrugged noncommittally. "I'm open to suggestions."

Stephanie pointed to the ocean. "I'm headed to the beach. Do a little light reading, maybe some swimming. You are welcome to join me if you like." She felt a flare of nervousness tickle her stomach. She wasn't sure what she'd do if he declined.

"Sounds great." He grinned at her.

Her relief was immediate and intense. So was the surge of anxiousness that made her flush pink from head to toe.

Stephanie led the way down to her cabana, trying to remember that they had been close once. Make-out in public close. But it had been pretend. Had their friendship?

"This is it." Stephanie gestured widely to cabana number 17.

"Fantastic." He plunked himself down on one of the lounge chairs and adjusted his hat.

Stephanie sat down, laughing and shaking her head. She pulled a paperback book out of her bag and got comfortable, preparing to slip right back into her daily routine.

"You're joking, right?" He laughed. Stephanie looked up to find his icy eyes twinkling with laughter.

"What?" She asked.

"A real book? Like, honest to goodness paper and ink? People still read those?"

Stephanie nodded. "Absolutely. I'll take paper over a digital screen any day of the week. You can't beat the way a book feels in your hands. Or the smell."

Devon raised an eyebrow at that. As a demonstration, she delicately sniffed the pages, offering him the book when she was done.

"Older books are better," she declared with a hint of lament in her tone. "They've done something to the ink."

With a grin, he shook his head, slumped down in the lounge chair and tipped the hat over his eyes as though he were going to take a nap.

"I trust you. But really, you must be the only hold out left."

"And proud." She muttered, a tiny smile pulling her lips up.

A couple of chapters later, Stephanie put the book away. Unsure if Devon was really napping or just faking it, she shimmied out of her sundress and paused a couple of steps from the cabana.

"I'm going in the water. You coming?"

Devon tipped the hat back away from his face, one squinted eye taking in her bikini-clad body.

"Nope. Have fun." He curled his lips up.

"Suit yourself." Stephanie half-jogged toward the water and then waded in, the cool salty sting refreshing and familiar. She swam out to a buoy at the edge of the safe swim zone, then back toward shore, noticing that Devon appeared to be watching her. She completed her usual 20 laps and dragged herself out of the water, the sugary sand warm and soft between her toes as she made her way back toward the cabana.

"Looks like you do that a lot." Devon said, eying her appreciatively.

Stephanie nodded and toweled herself off. "Nice of you to notice." It was. It really was. "I love to swim, do it every day I can. It's a good outlet."

Devon nodded, and looked back toward the water. There was no shortage of nearly-nude bathing beauties, but none seemed to hold his attention. She wasn't sure how to feel about that, but her body was on board with whatever she decided as long as it was somewhere in the neighborhood of thrilled.

Stephanie sat back down and realized she had never eaten her sandwich.

"Hungry?" She asked him.

"*Starving*. I thought you would never ask."

"You could have said something." Stephanie laughed at him.

"Nah. I was having too much fun pretending to sleep while you looked at that antiquated reading device. Slices of dead trees for heaven's sake." He shook his head.

"Funny guy." Stephanie teased, delighted that their natural friendly banter was still intact and this time nobody was watching. It could be organic and real and she didn't have to fake a damn thing.

It was terrifying.

And exhilarating.

She pulled her sundress back over her damp bathing suit and quickly combed out her wet hair before tying it up into a ponytail.

"How do people stay at the beach all day? I never understood it." Devon shook his head as they walked back up toward the shops and restaurants from the beach.

"I'm good for a couple of hours, then I'm done." Stephanie agreed.

"Exactly! It's hot, you get sticky and sand everywhere and the water is salty." Devon shook his head. "I don't get it."

Stephanie laughed at him. "You make a terrible Californian. What do you feel like eating?"

Devon thought about it, looking around at the signs above the assorted eclectic shops. He zeroed in on the pub.

"Feel like a beer?" He asked, waggling his dark eyebrows at her playfully.

"Why not."

They took a seat on the patio of O'Malley's and a petite waitress with black hair and shockingly bright blue eyes named Shannon took their drink order.

"How long are you here?" Stephanie asked, watching Devon watch their waitress.

The fact that it mirrored their first fake date amused her. To be fair, both waitresses were very cute and both had great asses.

She was woman enough to admit that—attractive is attractive no matter who you are.

"Just today." His eyes were still on Shannon's tiny but firm backside.

"That's not a vacation, Devon. That's a day off."

He shrugged, that eternal playful grin on his lips as he finally brought his eyes to hers.

"I'm apparently no good at vacation, either."

Shannon dropped off Stephanie's regular order—a Blue Moon with a slice of orange on the rim of the glass. Devon's Guinness looked positively black in contrast.

Devon's tone went a bit serious.

"So. Where have you been, Steph? I haven't seen you around town."

Stephanie debated how open she wanted to be.

"I haven't been in the city much," she replied, taking a deep drink of her beer, eyes watching people on the street for a moment before returning to Devon's face, which was entirely too genuinely interested in what she was saying. "Lying low. Doing vacation properly."

He laughed and nodded. "Fair enough."

There was a companionable silence as they both did a little people watching.

"This is nice," Devon said earnestly, relaxing into the patio chair. "No cameras, no pressure, no need to put on the game face. I see why you excel at doing vacation right."

Stephanie nodded, toying with some condensation on her glass with a fingertip. She offhandedly noticed a smear of canary paint near her cuticle.

"Going back to the city seemed like a very wrong choice after doing this for a while."

After finishing their first beers, they ordered dinner and had another round of drinks.

"I'm sorry." Devon said, all of a sudden and with a very serious expression on his face.

"What for?" Stephanie asked, eyebrows drawn together in confusion.

"Not calling. Texting. Saying hello or really anything after that day." He shook his head and pushed some shepherd's pie around in the dish. "That wasn't right. We were … friends. Or something like it."

Stephanie smiled and nodded. "Yes, we were. I'm glad you felt like we were too. It's okay. And really, you didn't have a choice. If our phone records had been pulled, or if you had been spotted texting me, there would have been media speculation about why. I didn't reach out either, for all the same reasons." Stephanie's brow creased. "You were paying me to act like I was your girlfriend. We completed the contract. I got paid, you moved on with your life. That's how it's supposed to go, honestly."

They sat there for a moment, regarding one another. Stephanie felt as though his sharp blue stare was peering into her darkest thoughts.

Finally, he broke the stare and gave a short, unenthusiastic nod.

"I guess." He pushed his plate aside and smiled. "Well, at least we got to have today, right?"

Stephanie agreed. "Absolutely."

THE PAIR SAT and talked for another few hours, Stephanie feeling like she finally had someone besides poor Maxwell that she could unload on. She didn't let on that she was living just upstairs, or where she had been 'vacationing' all this time, but she suspected that Devon could guess that it was nearby. As the waitstaff was putting down the umbrellas for the night, the pair stood and prepared to go their separate ways.

"Well, Stephanie, I had a fantastic day. Thanks for running into me on the street and then keeping me company and showing me the proper procedure for vacation." He tossed a substantial tip on the table, a reward for keeping them in beer and not fussing over them even though it was clear Shannon had recognized Devon immediately. The whole staff was already fairly immune to Stephanie, which was lovely.

They walked slowly down the block toward the hotel where Devon had left his car.

"My pleasure, Devon. Try to take more than a single day, next time though. It's much more satisfying."

"I'll try."

He nodded and opened his arms wide, inclining his head as though asking permission before bringing her into a warm friendly hug. She needed it much more desperately than she realized. Breathing in his ozone and earth scent nearly undid her.

"Drive safely." She managed to get out, making herself break the embrace before she did something embarrassing.

She waved as he started the car and drove away, back toward the city she would never again think of as home.

CHAPTER
Sixteen

STEPHANIE FOUND HERSELF resisting the urge to call Devon nearly every day. Frustrated with herself, feelings warring with one another in her mind and heart she tried to throw herself back into her painting.

Her normal abstracts based on nature began to turn into silhouettes. She found one piece, in particular, began to resemble Devon's side profile with uncanny accuracy. Deciding that it was at least a healthy outlet after much debate, she continued with the project, wondering if her lingering feelings of attraction would go away with the artistic purging.

They didn't.

Instead, she called Maxwell, and that only added to her frustration.

"Alright, out with it. Something's wrong." She demanded when he answered the call, not even pausing for a greeting.

"Hello, Lovely. To what do I owe the honor of this call?"

"I'm worried about you. Something's up and you're not talking. Spill."

Maxwell chuckled. "Where are you right now?"

"My apartment."

He clucked his tongue. "Shame. I'd happily bring Mr. Woo's if you were closer and we could chat all about it. Sadly, I don't have the time to drive to Santa Barbara and the food would be mostly inedible by the time I got there."

"I can always come to you. Tomorrow?"

Maxwell grunted. Stephanie's nerves jangled. Something was wrong with her friend, and he was keeping secrets.

They didn't keep secrets. Not from each other.

"Maxwell." She said quietly, pleading with her voice.

Finally, Maxwell sighed. "God, you're just the *worst*, Alex."

Stephanie said nothing, she just waited for him to start talking.

"Fine. I made partner—congrats to me, right? Except… now that I have it, I don't want it."

"Why not?"

"It sounds so ridiculous and selfish. So… spoiled."

"You're not really any of those things, Max. You know that, right?"

He sighed again, and Stephanie could picture him scrubbing a hand over his face. "I'm tired of being a lawyer, Alex. I don't even deal with terrible people for a living. I deal with contracts and paperwork and I'm just…" breath left him in a sigh again. "I'm starting to hate it."

Stephanie's heart tugged for her friend. "Tell your dad that, Max. He'll understand. He loves you."

"It's complicated, Lovely. I'll figure it out."

There was a pause. "What do you want to do instead?"

Maxwell laughed, and his laugh without the warm edge sounded very strange indeed.

"I don't even know. I just know I need something different. I really had fun designing your security app. Maybe there's something there for me. I'm clearly having my quarter-life crisis. And I thought that I had already done that—it's why I bought the Roadster and the Rolex."

Stephanie couldn't help but bark a laugh. "My profound apologies friend. If it makes you feel any better, I'm right there with you. I can totally relate. Take a vacation." She commanded. That seemed to be a running theme lately with the men in her life.

Wait. Was Devon once again a man in her life? She guessed the answer was yes, but needed to evaluate what exactly that might mean. She returned her focus to Maxwell.

"Go somewhere. See something. You'll figure it out. And that security app kicks ass—I can't even begin to understand how you make something like that. I'm sure there are options for you there." Stephanie thought for a moment. "Does Olivia have anything to do with this?"

There was silence for just a beat too long. He didn't try to deny it.

"Come on, Max. Let her *go*. Like all the way. Elsa level, ice demon chasing her down the mountain *gone*."

"Why do you know so much about Disney movies?" He chuckled at her. She was not about to get distracted, though.

"Who doesn't know about Frozen? Who doesn't love Disney movies? Do I need to drag you to the parks? I'm more than happy to do that. Hatter's Teacups seem like an excellent way to get you to relax."

"Oh god, no. Please. Torture me any other way." He chuckled again, but she could hear the falseness in it.

"Maxwell."

He sighed.

"I hear you, Alex. Yes, Olivia is part of it. She keeps popping up at the strangest times. Like she's following me around or something. There are always photographers in tow too. It makes no sense really. Paparazzi are not interested in me. She had me, she slept with James, she lost me. It's not complicated. If she'd just have focused on being with me, she'd still *be* with me."

Stephanie's heart broke just then. Her friend was hurting. And there she was, playing the hermit painter hours away—she couldn't even just get in her car and go give him a hug without it taking more than two hours of travel.

There were few downsides to living outside Los Angeles, but this was a big one, she realized.

"I love you, Max. Do the things that you need to do. Don't worry about your dad or the ex-girlfriend. This is about you." She thought, glancing out the window. "Can I do anything? Will bacon help?"

Maxwell chuckled and then sighed again. "No, sweet Alex. I'm okay."

Stephanie didn't believe him for a second, and the moment they hung up, she threw together an overnight bag and got in her car.

She drove as fast as she dared toward the city lights, and just a couple of hours later, she was on his stoop with Mr. Woo's and a sympathetic smile.

She knew that he would probably deny it outright if ever asked, but there had been tears in his eyes as he brought her in for a long, tight hug, she'd seen them glittering there in the porch light.

They said very little, eating the Chinese and sitting on his leather couch watching movies. Before she headed off to his guest room, he tugged her in for another embrace and kissed her hair before leaning his cheek on the top of her head.

"Thank you." He said.

She squeezed him back harder, tears in her own eyes. "Of course, Max. Any time. Always."

He seemed a bit lighter in the morning, and Stephanie headed back to the beach, but not until he promised to keep her posted on what was going on and not worry about what Samuel thought about his necessary life changes or what mess Olivia kept trying to deliver to his doorstep.

A WEEK AFTER meeting Devon on the street, Stephanie took her bag, bought a sandwich and went to her cabana, determined to enjoy what few weeks were left of the glorious Summer heat and sun. All too soon the water would become nearly too cold to swim in, though she doubted it would stop her. Offhandedly, she started to wonder if the hotel where Devon had parked would let her pay for pool time.

She was holding up a new paperback romance, staring over it and into the ocean instead of reading when the sound of someone sitting in the chair not four feet from her side startled her.

"What the hell—"

"Thought I might find you here." Devon gave a positively devilish grin and winked at her.

Stephanie felt heat rise into her cheeks, stomach rolling with nerves.

"This is my cabana. What are you doing here?" She feigned indignation.

"I'm trying out another vacation day."

"Just a day? We discussed this."

Devon shrugged. "More than that is too much of a commitment right now. I'm going to do a day and see how I feel."

Stephanie relented but quirked her mouth at him as if to shame him some. "Weirdly, I can relate to that."

They fell into an easy silence, Devon watching the waves and Stephanie trying and failing to read her book. Finally, she gave up and stripped off the gauzy blue sundress she was wearing, the red with white polka-dot bikini underneath.

"Swim?" She prompted.

Devon shook his head. "Nope."

Stephanie shrugged and strode toward the water, feeling his eyes on her back.

She did her 20 laps between the safe swim zone buoys, then joined him back at the cabana.

As she dried off, she looked at him. He was unabashedly watching her. She enjoyed that, very much.

"Hungry?" She asked, trying to sound confident, though his stare made her a little self-conscious.

"You bet."

Stephanie tried to pretend that the double entendre didn't send a zing of heat through her veins, but there was no denying it.

Instead of returning to the pub, Stephanie led him a few blocks over to a place she had found that had amazing sushi.

"You remembered." He smiled at her, holding the door open for her.

"Of course." She smiled back at him.

They found themselves falling into casual conversation about things that don't matter at all but make up everyone's lives as they used chopsticks to bring artfully rolled seafood and rice to their mouths. They were laughing and enjoying themselves and Stephanie hadn't felt so good or so light in months.

It was hard being Stephanie Von Feldt when it came to relationships, and at that moment, she realized that she had very much been missing simple friendship in her life. She'd gotten a taste with Devon before, and the temptation with Nora, but had never gotten a good chance to hang on to it with anyone but Maxwell.

She had burned through girlfriends through her young adult years because she couldn't tell when someone simply wanted to be her friend and when they wanted to be her friend because of her name, her parents, her connections. Stephanie's heart had been broken quite badly for the very same reasons, in fact.

It would seem she was tired of running from anything that felt real. She was jumping into this warm feeling Devon brought with both feet.

After lunch, they did a bunch of window shopping, Devon playing around with some floppy straw beach hats, Stephanie laughing so hard she couldn't catch her breath.

Stephanie picked up some tiny blown glass clownfish salt and pepper shakers from a wizened old woman street vendor. They were adorable, and would look good on her kitchen counter, she decided. They bought ice cream bars from a man who spoke no English and pushed around a cart full of treats with a bell on the handle.

It was late afternoon when Devon suggested he get back to the city.

"I had a great time." Stephanie smiled warmly at him. "Really. Thanks."

"Me too." He gave her the million-dollar smile and she felt her knees get a little weak. "This vacation thing is growing on me."

"I told you, one day is not a vacation."

Stephanie's heart sped up as he reached casually for her, lightly gripping her neck and planting a soft kiss on her forehead before waving and climbing into his car.

She managed to wave as he drove away, her breath sounding loud in her ears. Did he have any idea what he was doing to her? Was there any chance that she was doing the same thing to him?

DEVON TURNED UP at the cabana just as Stephanie was beginning to give up on him showing. He had come the previous two weeks as well, so this time Stephanie had prepared for him to come and had hoped he would show. Like a lovesick teenager, she had let her thoughts wander to him all too often as she painted, or tried to read, or attempted to do just about anything and failed because she was so distracted.

"What would you do if I weren't here?" She asked him as he settled down into the beach seat.

He shrugged, a playful look on his face.

"Probably hang out for a few minutes so I didn't look like a total weirdo and grab a bite to eat or something before driving back home." He pretended to think, hands laced together behind his head, his posture that of a completely relaxed Devon.

"That's the ultimate in vacation fail." She commented.

He shrugged. "Told you, I'm no good at it."

Stephanie laughed, feeling as though she too could relax now that he had arrived and their playful conversation was just as comfortable as it had always been.

"I've been doing laps all week. I'm good if we don't go in the water. You want to get off this beach and do something else?"

Devon nearly jumped out of the chair. "Yes. I thought you'd never ask."

"You just got here; I just needed a moment to get around to it."

Stephanie shook her head and gathered her things, following his long-legged stride back up to the street.

They spent another lazy day window shopping, talking, wandering around the city. At one point they got in Devon's car and just took a drive along the Highway 1, aimless, letting the wind blow through their hair as the salt air soaked into their skin.

"Why does this relax you so much when sitting on the beach doesn't?" Stephanie asked as they slowed for a curve.

Devon shrugged. "No idea. But this is one of the most beautiful places I have ever seen." He paused and put on a genuine smirk. "The company isn't bad either."

"I'm all aglow with your compliments." She teased back.

He stole a look at her, and his eyes were serious for a change. His hand reached out and took hers.

"No, really, Stephanie. I haven't had this good a time in years. The company couldn't be better."

She felt her stomach clench and heart speed up. Was he being honest? Playing with her? Acting? Stephanie hated that she couldn't always trust her impressions of people, especially those in the business and even more especially those she had worked with.

Going with honesty, she could feel a blush creep into her cheeks.

"I completely agree."

He smiled back at her and they drove into the wind.

AFTER A LONG drive, Devon looked rugged and wind-blown and sexy as hell and Stephanie just felt disheveled. She talked him into parking the car in front of the pub.

"I was thinking maybe a steak for dinner. Surf and turf?" he said, eyes nervously shifting from the Pub's sign back to Stephanie. "Can we go somewhere else? Do you mind?"

Stephanie shook her head and started to dig around in her bag for her house keys.

"Not at all. Can I change first?"

"Oh. Sure." Devon smiled and began walking in the direction of the hotel.

"No, this way." Stephanie laughed, gesturing to the

nearly invisible glass doorway between the pub's patio and the clothing store.

Devon shot her a questioning look.

"You're going to…buy a new outfit?" He stuffed his hands casually into his pockets, eyebrows drawn together.

She shook her head. "Nope. Just come with me." Stephanie pulled open the glass door and then led him up the staircase.

"Huh." He said as she put her key into the apartment door. "Unexpected."

As she pushed open the door and gestured for him to go in ahead of her, she got nervous. Aside from the very short time he had been in her parents' house while she put flowers in water on their first date, he had never seen her apartment, nor she his. This was a whole new level of personal space she was sharing.

"Wow." He sighed, standing and looking all around himself. "This is awesome." He spun to look at her. "You live here? Like permanently?"

Stephanie nodded and told him to make himself at home while she stepped into the bathroom to freshen up and then behind the screens of her bedroom to change into a slightly less casual dress, and actual underthings.

"These paintings are great," He called. Stephanie peeked around a screen and saw he was looking at the ones that flanked the TV. "Alex Felton. That's so weird. There's a huge painting of his at the Wilshire. It's like a magnet. I have to stop and look at it for at least five minutes every time I go into the hotel." He turned to look at her as she emerged from her bedroom in a casual but clean-lined Vera Wang frock. She had left 95% of her 'work' or 'dressy' clothing at her parents' house but was thankful she had grabbed a few of her favorites for occasions such as this.

"So, you like it?" She prompted, pulling on some ballet slippers for shoes as she walked back toward Devon. "The painting at the Wilshire?"

He nodded, an interesting fire blazing behind his icy blue eyes.

"It draws me in, every time I see it. I find something else in it, something new, to look at. Just great colors, interesting brushwork … " His hands stopped the wide gesticulations he had been making in the air. Devon looked a bit chagrined and dropped his gaze. "I sound like an art nerd."

She laughed.

"No, it's nice. I've actually never met anyone I could talk about paintings with." For the time being, she let it ride that he assumed the paintings were done by a man named Alex Felton. She had devised the pseudonym for her artwork for a number of reasons and was pleased that it was working.

"Ready?" He gave her another totally smoldering smile.

"Ready."

They drove across town to a very fancy steak house and Stephanie prepared herself as though she would have to brace for the flashbulbs of paparazzi cameras as they pulled up to the valet. It was as Devon was offering her his hand as help out of the car that she remembered that such a thing wouldn't be happening there. Her whole body relaxed as they walked to the host stand.

"What's wrong? Your whole face and body just… changed." Devon leaned in to ask as they were led to a quiet booth off to one side of the maroon and mahogany themed dining room.

Stephanie shook her head and smiled at the waitress as they gave their drink order after being seated. She mentally applauded and noted his observational skills.

"Nothing's wrong. I just was remembering that we're not in L.A.—I was gearing up for 'the smile' and all the bright lights."

Devon's eyes seemed to bore into hers, his expression kind and open.

"It's nice not to have to do that."

Stephanie nodded her agreement and glanced at the menu.

"I love it here. I don't run into many photographers trying to get inappropriate or awkward angle bikini pictures. I don't usually have to worry about running into photographers, period." Stephanie amended, closing her menu and taking in Devon's bright eyes and sharp, handsome features with her full attention. "That's why I've been on vacation for so long. It's quite relaxing."

"So, it seems." He grinned at her. "It looks good on you, anyway."

The waitress returned with their cocktails—a vodka and cranberry juice for Stephanie and a dark German beer that was impossible to pronounce without spitting a bit, for Devon.

They just looked at each other for a moment. Finally, Devon's black eyebrows drew together, and he seemed almost shy as he started to speak.

"You know, you're very different on vacation, Stephanie Von Feldt." He reached for her hand across the expanse of white linen tabletop. Heart picking up, she met him halfway and his warm fingers folded around hers. The contact electrified her insides.

"How's that?" She asked, head tilted to one side, her stomach doing flips and heart rate increasing as he brushed her knuckles with his thumb.

"When I ran into you on that sidewalk? I didn't recognize you at first. Here was this bronzed goddess with wild Medusa hair and the most fantastic knockout body."

"You couldn't see through my dress, and my hair was up." Stephanie couldn't help but chuckle.

Undeterred, he smiled and continued, his penetrating blue stare locked on her amber eyes. Stephanie very nearly trembled as his thumb repeatedly grazed her knuckles. She had a moment to wonder if he knew what that simple touch was doing to her.

"I could see that through your dress with the sunlight behind you, thank you very much, and your hair is gorgeous and wild no matter how you try to contain it." He leaned a little closer to her over the table. "My point is, that just then, I realized that vacation Stephanie was quite possibly the most beautiful woman I had ever set my eyes on. It would have been foolish of me to try and spend the day without her after I had so carelessly knocked her over."

Stephanie's pulse pounded in her ears. She took a moment to mull his honesty. There was no indication that he was being anything but genuine. Stephanie took a few breaths to slow her heart rate—and libido—down a bit.

"I don't know what to say, Devon." She said quietly. "That's without a doubt the best compliment and come-on line I have ever heard."

He smiled as though she had chosen just the right response.

"Steph, it's all true." He lifted her hand to his lips and gently kissed the knuckles he had been softly tantalizing.

She gave him a gentle and sincere smile as they just watched one another for a moment. She wanted to believe it all, quite desperately. So, she did.

The arrival of their meals interrupted the moment, and their conversation lightened considerably as Stephanie made her way through lobster and the most decadently tender filet mignon she had ever eaten. Devon put away his own ribeye with reckless abandon, proclaiming it the food of the gods and leaving nothing on his plate.

"Dessert tonight?" the waitress prompted, hopeful smile on her young, beautiful face.

Stephanie smiled back and asked for some of their famed chocolate mousse torte to take home.

"See? One more reason you're doing vacation right." Devon chuckled.

"Just one more reason I have to swim 20 laps every day, you mean."

After he had paid the check, they navigated their way back out of the restaurant. As they waited for the valet to retrieve Devon's car, he lightly gripped her with a hand on her waist.

"Thank you, Devon. That was fantastic." Stephanie looked up at him.

"You're welcome, Stephanie." He gazed down on her, admiration laced with lust painting his features. Stephanie could feel her heart skip.

For a moment time stopped. Devon's other hand rose to the side of her face and he leaned in to kiss her. It was light, sweet, and set Stephanie's whole body on fire. She very nearly needed help remaining vertical as her knees threatened to buckle in his embrace.

The sound of a throat clearing broke them apart.

"Sorry. Sir? Your keys?" The embarrassed valet offered the keyring to Devon, who tipped him heavily and then went back for another passionate taste of Stephanie before leading her to the car.

She laughed as they got a round of applause from the other valets and some of the customers who were likewise waiting for their cars.

Devon was the one to break the somewhat awkward silence on the short ride back to Stephanie's apartment.

"So…why was that so different from when we were pretending?" He asked.

Stephanie heaved a silent sigh of relief, glad that it had been different for him too. What if it hadn't been? She might have died from embarrassment.

"We were pretending." She said simply. "You know as well as I do that movie and TV kissing is not the same as the real thing."

He nodded, then, his perpetual sense of humor shining through, he raised his eyebrows.

"Thank God, for that. I might have been into you for millions of dollars before I was able to break it off."

Stephanie laughed. "That's actually almost as flattering as what you said at dinner."

"I'm just full of grandiose statements." He joked, pulling the parking brake as they had pulled up at the pub.

"Coming up?" She asked, her voice sounding much lower than usual. Her level of desire for him was frightening and exhilarating.

"Absolutely. You're not getting to eat that whole piece of cake all by yourself."

Feeling lighter than air, Stephanie led him into her loft. She put the cake in the fridge for later.

"Need a drink or anything?" She asked over her shoulder, his attention once again on the paintings next to the TV.

"Sure. Whatever you have is fine."

Stephanie nodded and brought him a bottle of beer from her refrigerator. She stood next to him as he very seriously studied her paintings.

"What do you see?" she asked quietly, watching his face as he responded.

"These are complicated." He took a drink from the bottle and then tilted his head to one side as though contemplating. "The layers of blue and green make me think of water, but then there's that distracting red and yellow. Sunrise over the ocean maybe?" He quirked his mouth to one side and squinted just a bit to help him see better.

Stephanie stayed quiet. They were the pieces she had done over the time he was visiting his family when they were pretending to be a couple. For her, they were a purge of emotions. Blue and green her calm state, the crimson and goldenrod the flares of like and even lust that she had to package away while he was paying her to be his girlfriend.

Stephanie's mind flitted to how they would negotiate that aspect of their past if they became a couple for real, then she shrugged it off. Vacation romances tended to stay on vacation. No use overthinking them.

"How is it that you came to own this pair of Alex Felton paintings?" Devon graced her with a playful grin and pulled her down onto the sofa with him.

"I know someone with connections." Stephanie said. The half-truth settled darkly in her gut.

"Mmmm. I might need a referral." Devon sat his beer on the table, removed Stephanie's from her hand and set it down as well.

Slowly, he traced the contours of her face with his fingertips, his lips mere inches from hers. It was slow torture. He pulled her hair down from the bindings she had put it in and let it be wild and loose around her face. Stephanie's skin felt like he was leaving trails of fire with his touch, her pulse racing and breath beginning to quicken. Finally, he placed his mouth on hers and stole her very breath with a kiss so sweet and luxurious and devastating that she never wanted to have to come up for air. One of his hands lightly gripped the back of her head, fingers twisting gently in her hair.

Stephanie's mind went blank as he teased her bottom lip with his tongue and she allowed herself to open to him, their tongues dancing and stroking and exploring, a burning ache beginning to form in Stephanie's lower abdomen.

"Holy shit." Devon was nearly panting when they finally broke for air.

"Agreed." Stephanie said, laughing in embarrassment as she leaned her forehead forward on his shoulder. It had indeed been a while. He cradled her gently.

"I swear my motives were pure with dinner. I just wanted to get to know you better."

"And so, you have." Stephanie laughed, lifting her head. She peered into his stunning blue eyes. "How well do you want to know me?" She asked saucily, a bit shocked at her own brazenness.

Devon gave a belly laugh, but his voice was low with desire.

"That's a loaded and foolish question, Ms. Von Feldt." He growled playfully, sweeping down for another passionate kiss that left them both breathless.

"Come on then. Let me show you the view of the ocean at night from this side of the loft."

Stephanie stood, extended her hand to him and then pulled him with her toward the bedroom.

"If you feel like this is rushing things—"

Stephanie shushed him with her fingers, leading him by the hand all the way to the windows.

True to her word, there was the most amazing view of the ocean by moonlight outside the floor-to-ceiling windows.

"That's amazing." Devon whispered.

"My permanent vacation is pretty incredible," Stephanie said, her tone just as soft. With a flip of a switch, the glass became nearly opaque. "We can see out, but nobody can see in."

"That's a good idea, as close as your bed is to these gigantic windows."

Standing on her tiptoes, she reached for him again, wrapping her arms around his neck, his encircling her waist. He devastated her with another delving kiss, then lit her aflame as he kissed his way down her neck to the curve of her shoulder, hand carefully lowering the zipper on her dress as he kissed his way down her collarbone.

With a gentle brushing motion, the straps fell from her shoulders and the dress hit the floor.

"They're nuts not to want this body on screen all the time." He shook his head, admiring the toned physique in front of him. "But I'm perfectly happy to keep this visual all to myself."

Seeing the pure admiration and lust in his eyes put Stephanie strangely at ease. Because of how she had been labeled, she had suffered a love/hate relationship with her tight and obvious stomach muscles, the powerful thighs and calves that swimming had bestowed upon her, and of course the broad and strong shoulders she had no end of trouble finding designer blouses to cover. Most designers wouldn't dress a girl that couldn't fit a sample size, and Stephanie was definitely not a sample size.

She gently tugged his shirt out of the waistband of his pants and took her time undoing the buttons, pressing her skin against him. Devon groaned and took her mouth with his, his arousal evident against the press of her body.

As soon as his shirt was off, Devon walked them both toward the bed, lips as many places on Stephanie's face and neck as he could get them.

As her legs hit the mattress, she stopped, consuming his mouth with hers as her fingers carefully undid the button on his linen pants, her mouth only leaving his to taste his chest as her hands pushed both his pants and boxers to below his hips.

She took a moment to marvel at the lithe chest and stomach muscles under her lips and hands. Devon had a sparse sprinkling of dark hair on his chest, but other than that his skin was soft and smooth and ten shades lighter than it should be for someone who lived in such a sunny place. Good for someone playing the undead, however, which he was.

"You should get out in the sun more often." She teased quietly.

"Oh really? I think I know someone who spends a lot of time at the beach. Maybe I'll plan on a long vacation."

"Mmmm. That would probably be a good idea."

Devon cradled her head with one of his large hands, a playful grin on his lips, icy blue eyes twinkling at her. He dipped in for a soft kiss, then another, then one that left them both breathless and clawing to remove Stephanie's lacy bra. After a few moments of tangled limbs and harsh breaths, Stephanie opened her eyes and realized she couldn't recall how they had ended up horizontal on her bed.

"Still time to call things off." Devon said playfully, hovering above her with that troublemaker smile before making her squirm as he took one breast and then the other into his hot mouth and nibbled, then blew on them, making them contract into even tighter points.

"Not a chance." She sighed, her brain very rapidly losing the ability to think clearly or form coherent speech.

Devon's mouth plundered hers once more, her hips rising to his in automatic response to his close proximity. He worked his way down her front, leaving a hot wet trail of kisses as he went, Stephanie horrified to hear herself moaning like a wanton teenager.

He hooked his fingers into the barely-there waistband of her panties and slid them down her hips and legs, teasing her sensitive thighs with his mouth as he went.

"Please," She said to him as he paused, his gaze fraught with lust and desire. "Before I die." He laughed at her and retrieved a condom from his pants. "Really?" It was her turn to tease. "Are you a boy scout, Mr. Greene?"

She tensed a bit despite her joking. It had been a very, *very* long time since she had been intimate with someone. But she wanted this. Probably too much.

"Definitely not a scout, but prepared just in hopes. You have *no idea* how hopeful I was." He kissed her again, Stephanie's thoughts losing all structure as he pressed against her opening with his hot silky arousal and teased the tight bundle of aroused nerves at the juncture of her thighs with his fingers.

Her need becoming urgent, she pressed her hips into his once more and with a smooth adjustment, he entered her in a slow but firm thrust that very nearly had her up and over the peak of an orgasm in just that motion.

"Jesus, Stephanie." He whispered into her neck as he began a careful rhythm.

Stephanie rocked her hips in time with his as if they had done this hundreds of times before. He was so firm and hot inside her, her body responding with what felt like a liquid clenching of muscles. As she felt the pressure building somewhere low in her belly, Stephanie wrapped her legs around his hips and called his name, her climax sudden and overwhelming.

As she tried to remember how to breathe, she could feel Devon coming close to his own peak. Finding enough coherency to grip him tighter with her legs and angle her body into his so that he could go even deeper inside her, she cried out once more as the world spun away from her and they both found their release within breaths of one another.

For a moment, they panted together, then Devon chuckled, a sound low in his throat. He planted a gentle kiss on her mouth, then her cheek and finally her neck, before carefully extricating himself from her tightly clenched body and rolling off to the side.

Stephanie's world was all heartbeat and gasping for air and sensations in places she had forgotten existed. It was a delicious ache that she felt in her most private parts, and it made her smile.

When the world made sense again, she turned onto her side and curled into Devon's body, his arm coming up to wrap around her shoulder, his hand idly caressing her back.

"Your vacation is awesome." He muttered.

Stephanie managed a short laugh.

"Not too shabby yourself, Mr. Greene. You may have been a little presumptuous in your preparations, but I'm not upset about it."

He kissed her forehead, taking her teasing in stride.

"I stand by my original statement—you have no idea how hopeful I was. I've been trying to figure out how to talk you into an actual date for weeks. Seems to me you're the vixen who demanded I see the view from her bedroom."

"Fair enough."

"I was right by the way."

"About what?" Stephanie asked.

"Your face, that day in Blu-Jam over the French toast? That was totally your O-face."

Stephanie laughed, and though she felt as though she should be embarrassed, she just couldn't manage to get there.

CHAPTER
Eighteen

THEY LAY THERE long enough to fall asleep, though that hadn't been Stephanie's intention. When she woke a few short hours later, Devon was peacefully sleeping next to her and they had somehow pulled the covers up over themselves.

As quietly as she could, Stephanie slipped from the bed and pulled on the first article of clothing she could locate, which happened to be Devon's dress shirt. She made a pit stop in the bathroom, then retrieved her flat beer from the coffee table before being drawn by her paints and canvases.

Using only a small Ott light, she felt the need flow through her body and onto one of her large canvases. This was her prime painting time, and the glorious recreation with Devon had loosed some kind of frenetic artistic energy.

As she was standing back, assessing what work had presented itself, she saw his shadow approaching.

"I wondered where you went." He said quietly, wrapping his arms around her, looking at her work over her shoulder. "I saw all this when we came in. You paint, I see?"

"Yes. I love it. It's been a big part of my life since I started this vacation. Actually, starting from around when I took you as a client."

"I like it." He said, nuzzling her neck and sending a whole new set of tingles down her spine.

Stephanie set the palette down, put her brushes into a cup of cleaning solution and turned to Devon, planting a kiss full of fresh need and desire on his mouth.

"Oh really? Like that, is it?" He smiled down at her.

"Yep." Stephanie turned off the light and led him back to the bed.

This time she took the lead, teasing and stroking his hot flesh with her hands and hair and mouth until he called out her name, voice edged with urgency and fear and want.

She retrieved another condom from the strip he had in his pants pocket and straddled him, taking him into her body one fraction at a time, seeing the pleasure and frustration in his eyes.

"You're killing me." He groaned.

"Shhh."

Finally, once he was seated fully inside her, Stephanie began a slow rhythm that made it feel as though he were touching every part of her.

Her sex history—though not extensive—had been relatively mundane compared to this, and never before had she felt the intense desire or need like she was with Devon. As she rocked her body against his, he caressed her breast with one hand, the other firmly gripping her ass to keep her in place.

"Don't stop." He whispered; eyes heavy-lidded. Stephanie smiled a wicked grin and promised that she wouldn't.

The heavy tingling sensation began to build and she increased her speed, Devon's hand moving from her breast to the nub of pleasure where they were joined. As he stroked the tight bundle of nerves, Stephanie felt herself fly into a million pieces, heard Devon call her name and felt him throb in time to her own climax and the slow descent back down again.

She leaned forward, head on his shoulder as they panted together.

"Holy Christ, you are trying to kill me."

"What a way to go." She breathed.

Stephanie carefully rolled away from him, skin flushed and tingling in the cool night air of her loft.

As they curled into one another once more, sated desires bringing drowsiness, Devon spoke softly, eyes locked on hers.

"You're amazing, Ms. Von Feldt. And if I may say so, I do believe you're at risk of making me fall in love with you. More this time around than last."

Stephanie's breath caught and her heart momentarily stopped.

"You sure that's not just the afterglow talking, Mr. Greene?"

His eyes penetrated hers, his features serious for once.

"Positive. I could fall devastatingly hard for you Ms. Von Feldt, and not even regret it. I think I knew that danger from the first time I saw you." His fingertips tracing the edges of her face, she could see truth in the icy depths of his eyes. "It was one of the first things I liked about you. It was like a tease though, or a challenge. I couldn't possibly fall in love with you when we were just acting out a scripted relationship. Especially not with my history with relationships. My three-date limit simply never allowed for anything like that. It was preposterous. Impossible." His mouth quirked that irresistible smirk. "But it's just one of those things—the more you fight it, the more at risk you are of giving in."

She stared at him, fighting the emotions warring within her.

Stephanie realized that she could easily fall for Devon too, and probably had been headed down that path for quite some time.

If she was really being honest, she'd admit that it started from that first date. Maybe even that first phone call where he seemed so nervous.

"I—"

He kissed her softly, cutting off the possibility of any kind of confession on her part. Perhaps he didn't need to hear it, or maybe he didn't want to. Maybe he was saving her from feeling obligated to put it out there as he had.

Somewhere the afterglow became the orange and yellow of dawn and they both fell into a very peaceful sleep.

STEPHANIE WOKE TO an empty space beside her in bed. She slipped from the sheets, pulled on a robe and headed toward the clanking and rumbling noise that was coming from the other end of the loft. Devon was in the kitchen attempting to figure out how to work her coffee pot.

He flashed her a slow, sexy smile as he saw her approaching.

"Good morning." He pulled her in for a kiss. "I need help. This damned machine is smarter than me."

Stephanie snuggled into his side, his arm around her shoulders.

"Me too. That's why I'm eternally grateful that the pub is open for breakfast and that I have this."

She pulled away from him and gestured to a nondescript metal box next to her microwave. Stephanie gently tugged on some rope and a door slid open in the front of the box.

"What is that?" Devon raised an eyebrow, curious.

"Dumbwaiter. Straight into the kitchen of the pub."

Devon's mouth dropped open, then he smiled and his eyes gleamed.

"That. Is. Genius."

Stephanie nodded, pulling out the pen and order-sheet that she kept inside the mini-fridge sized box at all times.

"I know. Best money I spent when I did the remodel."

They decided what they wanted for breakfast and wrote it down, as well as juice and coffee.

As Stephanie pressed a button that caused the box to descend with a hum of gears and motors, Devon laughed and said again, "No, really, that's the smartest thing I have ever seen. Probably ever."

He swept her up into a kiss and embraced her gently, looking into her eyes as they just stood there in the kitchen… being.

Before long the order hummed its way back up into Stephanie's kitchen and they were seated at the farmhouse table drinking coffee and eating breakfast. Devon eyed Stephanie seriously.

"You okay?" He asked. "Last night went … well, as hoped but not as planned, exactly."

"I'm fantastic. You?" She allowed herself thirty seconds of nervous heart pounding. Devon's easy smile as he took another forkful of waffles put her at ease.

"Never better."

After breakfast, Stephanie attempted to take a shower but was interrupted by Devon. After what could only be called acrobatic sex at its best mixed with water and soap and some of the most intense orgasms of her life, they both finally got clean and eventually ordered up lunch from the pub as well.

Devon started looking restless as the afternoon got long, however, and finally resorted to a pouty face as they lounged in the living room watching some inane movie in between what could only be referred to as groping sessions.

"What's wrong?"

"I don't want to go back to the city tonight." He mumbled into her hair.

"So, don't go. Tell the studio you got sick. Or hey, how about that you're on vacation?"

He smiled and nodded. "It's an idea. But I really have to be there for the shoot tomorrow."

They snuggled in a little closer until the movie was over.

Devon leaned into Stephanie and painted a slow kiss on her mouth that set every nerve in her body on fire. He swept her bottom lip, then her mouth with his skilled tongue, and before very long she found herself naked beneath him and welcoming him into her body with a quiet sigh. She wrapped her legs around him as he kissed her quite literally stupid, and the feel of him moving inside her drove them both to an explosive climax.

"So, you don't forget me when I go back to the city." He panted, gently kissing her neck as they both regained the ability to breathe and speak and think more clearly.

"Like there was a chance of that."

"Thank goodness." He kissed her once more on the mouth and they rose, dressing and trying to put some semblance of order back to their appearances.

They wandered slowly down to Devon's car once he had gathered all of his things and kissed slowly one last time before he reluctantly got into the drivers' seat.

"I'll call you." He said, leaning down so she could see him through the passenger side window.

"You'd better." She threatened, waving as he pulled away from the curb.

Stephanie made her way back up to her apartment, stiff and sore in places she had long forgotten that she had. A quiet smile lifted her lips as she locked the door behind her and she meandered over to her canvases.

Vacation had never been done quite so well in such a short period of time in her opinion.

CHAPTER Nineteen

STEPHANIE FOUND HERSELF falling into a comfortable, predictable routine over the next few weeks. She'd venture into Los Angeles to stay at Devon's modern, luxury condo for at least a couple of days during the week. Since he had a pretty steady shoot schedule, she had lots of free time but it wasn't a terrible thing.

More than once she went into town to replenish his groceries or just to see if the paparazzi were at all interested in her, by herself, out and about.

They were indeed interested, and took their fair share of photos and short videos, lobbing random questions like always, but they weren't nearly as focused on her as they seemed to be when she was attached to a client. Stephanie couldn't help but count that as a win for her previous client performances.

She knew that while it was very hush-hush, she was not the only one in town doing that kind of work. It was just one of those things. Kind of like Fight Club—rule number one is nobody talks about it. Everybody knows there are people out there, willing to fake date for money and publicity, but unless you know someone who knows someone in the know, you won't ever find out for sure who they are. And heaven forbid you accidentally spill the beans—you might go from on the rise to blacklisted immediately.

One afternoon she managed to catch the live broadcast of TMZ, and they were speculating about her 'disappearance'. She felt the smile grow on her face as the cast tossed ideas back and forth about her relationships and what she was up to.

"Wouldn't you like to know?" She had found herself laughing more than once. She rarely watched the gossip shows, but every now and then they were worthwhile. All her muscles tensed when they veered way off course and dredged up her ex-boyfriend. She nearly snapped the TV off in reaction but made her hand still on the remote.

"Jared Collins was her first serious relationship way back in the day—you remember that?" The host asked. There was some vague agreement. "He was so bad, too. Tried to use her name to get work, slept around on her, sometimes with her close girlfriends—"

"Not really friends, then." Someone piped up. Stephanie mentally fist-pumped the woman.

"—true, terrible friends. And when they split up he struggled and wasn't at all quiet about how it was her fault.

She kind of fell off the grid after that. I'd be guarded about dating too if I were her. Hard not to get attention with parents like hers. Seems like a sweet girl though—stays out of trouble, no major drama."

"You think she's hiding something?"

The host shrugged but was shaking his head. "Doesn't seem like it. I mean, she went out with Brett Masterson, right? Who would do that if they didn't really want to?"

There was a general chorus of laughter and Stephanie was finally able to breathe a little bit. Her past was back where it belonged and they weren't looking too hard at her relationships.

If nothing else, her parents were overjoyed at being able to see her more often, even if it was only for the day. Stephanie's skin felt strange every time she found herself in her parents' house, but never mentioned it. It was almost like the air pressure was different there somehow. She liked to think it was something similar to a butterfly having already emerged from her cocoon—you can't go back in; it will never be the same.

She also took advantage of being able to swing by and have lunch with Maxwell if he was between clients. Stephanie realized she was keeping herself purposely busy, but it felt good. *She* felt good and was trying not to look that gift horse in the mouth.

On the weekends Devon would drive out to see her, the magic of her beach-side permanent vacation home weaving its spell around them and their blossoming relationship. They had so far kept their coupledom a secret, and Stephanie was beginning to wonder how long that might hold up and how to go about handling it, especially after she popped up on TMZ as a hot discussion topic.

Much to her delight, Stephanie's artwork as Alex Felton had found a wide audience, and her list of commissioned pieces was getting quite lengthy. She had even sold to the hotel just down the street from her loft, three large pieces that were distributed between the lobby, restaurant, and lounge. When she and Devon were apart, she worked feverishly on her art, and when they were together, she set it aside for her time with Devon and her family. It was a strange dual life, but it was working well.

One weekend they had wandered down to one of the small bars on the beach to lounge and relax before Devon headed back into the city.

Stephanie had been in discussions with Marty earlier in the week about indefinitely suspending the business.

"You seem a little off today. You alright?" Devon asked, his eyes concerned.

Stephanie nodded, taking a sip of her cocktail.

"Sorry. I'm fine, just thinking about work stuff."

Devon's eyebrows shot up and he gave her that wolfish grin she had come to adore.

"Oh really? Thinking about getting back in the game?"

Stephanie laughed.

"Nope, nothing of the sort. I'm perfectly content being on vacation. I just have some paperwork issues to sort out."

Devon nodded, biting his bottom lip in a way that instantly had Stephanie's blood warming, her skin tingling with desire.

"I see. Anything I can help with?"

"Nope. Nothing at all. Thanks though." Stephanie leaned over and planted a soft kiss on his mouth.

"You're not going to pop up on TMZ dating anyone I know, are you?" He teased.

"Maybe." Stephanie teased back. At his fleeting look of horror that she might be serious, she laughed and shook her head. "No. I swear. Unless it's you that is. Actually, I've been trying to figure out the best way to mothball the business."

Devon seemed pleased, but then his eyebrows drew together again.

"Did I put you out of business, Stephanie?"

The look on his face made Stephanie laugh a loud, hearty belly laugh. He began to chuckle too but still seemed a little concerned.

"No, no you didn't. I did."

"Oh. Good. I think."

Stephanie took his hand.

"Come on, let's go back to my place and talk about it." She winked suggestively and he dropped some money on the table as she led him back to the loft by his hand.

Stephanie shed her dress the moment they were inside her loft, and to Devon's total surprise, there was not a stitch of clothing underneath it.

"Seriously?" He gaped.

"Yep."

She took off toward the bedroom like a gazelle, flipping the privacy switch on the windows before leaping into bed.

"Do you even know how awesome that is?" He asked her.

"Yep." She replied saucily. "Want to know what else?"

"Absolutely."

"How would you feel about not using condoms anymore?"

Devon was shimmying out of his clothes as quickly as he could but stopped dead. Eyes wide, his mouth curled into a slow smile. "Not nice to tease. I think I just died a little. You're serious?"

Stephanie nodded, seductively posed on the bed. "Protection by injection began a couple of weeks ago."

By the time he got to the bed and pressed his naked body on top of hers, they were both nearly aflame with desire, and he looked like an excited teenager.

"You're terrible." He mumbled, stroking her cheek with one hand before plundering her mouth with hot salty kisses.

"I thought I was amazing?" She teased back, lifting her hips in invitation.

"Well…" He kissed her breath away and entered her in one swift thrust, swallowing her moans with his mouth as they rocked together. "Oh my god. There's no way that this feels as fantastic as I think it does."

"Yes, there is." Stephanie replied breathlessly, shocked at how much difference that flimsy piece of latex could make.

Never had Stephanie been so aware of her body, so in tune with her sensations. Feeling his firm flesh inside her made her feel empowered and beautiful and wanted. The way he touched her inside and out when they made love left her feeling as though every single nerve ending in her body was at attention and singing.

As he pushed himself into her warm core, Stephanie could feel the heavy tingling beginning in her abdomen and pushed her hips into his. Time didn't matter anymore and the next time Stephanie was even partly coherent, they were both at the peak of their climax, crying out and then stiffening before collapsing into a sweaty heap of flesh and breath.

They lay there for a few moments, letting their bodies relax. Devon casually twisted a few strands of Stephanie's hair around his fingers, her head on his chest, his strong heartbeat thumping under her ear.

"Are you worried about closing down the business?" Devon asked quietly, his voice rumbling through his chest.

"No. Not really."

"Then why are you so wound up about it? And don't tell me you're not. I know you better than that, Steph."

Stephanie sighed and pulled herself to a sitting position.

"I'm not sure how to handle the information behind the job. Like the client list." She playfully pointed his direction.

"Just don't say anything at all." He shrugged matter-of-factly. "That's the simple answer, right?"

Stephanie's tension was creeping back in. She slipped from the sheets and began to hunt for a clean bathing suit. Despite the fact that the water was getting colder by the week, she felt the need to go swim off some of her stress so that she could work out how to have Marty and Samuel draw up the legal end.

"Is that okay with you? I mean, really okay?" She tugged on a navy-blue bikini and then pulled a sundress over her head.

Devon shrugged. "Why wouldn't it be?" He followed her example and began to tug his pants and shirt back on.

"You paid me. A significant sum of money. To pretend to be your girlfriend. Clearly, you weren't the only one. Isn't that strange? That at some point in our past I was your … employee?"

She could feel her eyebrows were pulled together, a grimace on her face. She hoped Devon didn't think it was disgust—it was discomfort. Pain even.

Devon swept her into his arms, cradling her face against his chest for a moment before planting a soft, but devastating kiss on her mouth.

"I don't even think of it like that, I swear. I adore you, Steph, I did even then. We met because I had to pay for some image enhancement, or whatever the hell my PR team called it. You came with the deal. I got to take you out and do some really fun things and act out a crazy fun break up scene with you at that premiere. But more importantly—" he framed her face with his hands, gazing deep into her eyes, which were now swimming with tears. "—I got to get to know you, and see you in that ridiculously HOT lace dress." Stephanie laughed, wiping at the couple of tears that escaped. "You need to wear that again, by the way, it was just…" he shrugged, biting his lip, lost for words, but Stephanie could feel a certain part of him pressing into her belly and that alone told her how he felt about the dress.

His baby blues were electric as he stared at her. That signature smirk showed up, and it seemed like something passed behind those thoughtful orbs. His hands moved down her body, forearms gently resting on her hips as he opened his mouth, then closed it again. Finally, he spoke. "I do believe I love you, Stephanie Von Feldt."

Stephanie's heart slowed in a dramatic way in her chest. Breath was hard to pull in for a moment, and then pure joy exploded throughout her body, lighting up every nerve with bright light as she realized that he meant it, and what was more, she was in love with him too. It was an oddly surprising discovery, but not unwelcome and not really all that shocking if she gave herself a moment to embrace the idea.

Stephanie felt the tension drain from her and she just hung there in his arms, Devon's hands tight on her bottom and keeping her upright. His lopsided grin gave her life.

"You love me, Mr. Greene?"

"I do. It's crazy, but I really do."

"That's lucky. Because I do believe you made me fall right back in love with you."

Devon's smile gave way to a toothy grin and he swooped down for a kiss that sucked the breath right out of her.

For what felt like quite a while they just stood there, holding one another and trying to figure out if it was really necessary to ever move again.

Finally, Stephanie broke the reverie.

"Thank you." She hugged him tight, relief and heavy happiness coursing through her veins. She should have known that Devon would find it appropriate to crack a joke.

"Does this mean you won't ever tell me who was a client and who wasn't?" He looked so crestfallen, she couldn't help the giggle that burst out of her.

Stephanie laughed in earnest and pulled away from him, heading toward the door.

"That was actually your suggestion if you recall."

"Maybe you could tell me in code? Like blink once for yes and twice for no?"

Stephanie shook her head, snatched up a towel and headed out the door, Devon racing to catch up to her before the door slammed shut in his face, still teasing her about finding out who the other men were in her life.

CHAPTER

Twenty

STEPHANIE KNEW THAT keeping her relationship with Devon a secret wouldn't last forever, but she had rather been enjoying their comfortable little bubble.

She had come with him into the city for Thanksgiving since it was her parents' big event for the year. They always threw an extravagant all day and sometimes multiple day party with what seemed like unlimited food and drinks and celebrities from way back when to up and coming wandering through at some point.

Marty didn't miss it for anything, and neither did Samuel. Naturally, Maxwell was always there as well. Despite the fact that Stephanie felt nearly completely disconnected from the Hollywood world, it was one of her very favorite times of the year and she couldn't find any good reason not to attend.

"My dad is … well, just don't let him push you around. He's a teddy bear, but I'm his only daughter."

They had pulled into the wide circular drive just before noon on Thanksgiving Day, Devon's silver VW navigating the already thick gathering of vehicles and pulling into the garage at Stephanie's instruction.

"Got it." He looked across the car at her. "You're nervous." It wasn't a question.

Stephanie sighed, adjusting her new Chanel dress, then checking her makeup in the mirror one more time.

"Yes. Mother likes me to be put together. And I've never brought home a boy before."

The corner of Devon's mouth lifted and he got out of the car, quickly opening her door. Once it was closed behind her, he pressed her up against the side of the vehicle and ravaged her mouth with a breath-stealing kiss.

"You're stunning."

"You messed up my lipstick." Her eyes were a bit distant because of the kiss, her lips swollen and rosy never-minding the smudged lipstick. Stephanie assessed the look in his eyes. It was pure lust, and she knew him well enough to know he was trying to calculate how much time they had. "You're wearing my lipstick. And no, we can't sneak off anywhere first."

Devon pouted, trying to sneak a warm hand up her thigh while he still had her captive.

"Shame, that."

Stephanie laughed and ducked under his arm and out the garage door.

"Cool off, Mr. Greene. We have to go meet my parents."

Devon made a show of straightening the collar on his button-down shirt, and wiping off the lipstick with his fingers, then extended his arm for Stephanie to link hers in.

"They're going to adore me, just like you do."

"Of course, they will." Stephanie leaned her head on his shoulder momentarily as they walked toward the front door.

Taking a deep breath, Stephanie rang the bell on her parent's house, strangely ashamed and curious about why she was feeling so nervous. Her parents had been nothing but supportive about her relationship, though they only knew who she was seeing by name. This was the first time they'd be meeting him in person.

Stephanie had told them that she was seeing someone, was very happy and even felt as though she had fallen very deeply in love.

"Oh, my darling! That's such wonderful news!" Marlowe had gushed over her peach sorbet.

Stephanie had chosen to tell them at one of their Malibu lunch dates.

"Fantastic, darling, when do we get to meet him?" Her father's warm eyes had soothed Stephanie. She hoped that he would approve of her choice.

"I'm not sure. He's got a very busy schedule. He's in the trades." She said, which earned a grave but understanding nod from both of her parents.

So, Thanksgiving it was.

Marlowe herself opened the heavy wooden door with a flourish.

"Stephanie! Darling!" She opened her arms wide and swooped down to hug her daughter in a breath of lavender and lemon. "And this! Who is this dashing young man?" Marlowe's eyes were twinkling as she took in Devon.

"Devon Greene, this is my mother, Marlowe Von Feldt. Mom, this is Devon."

Marlowe swept Devon up in the same broad squeeze that she had bestowed upon her daughter.

"It's my pleasure, surely." Marlowe grinned, hands up near her face in her usual gesture, the hundreds of tiny gold bracelets on her wrists gently clinking together as they fell down her arm. "Please, come in! Come in."

Devon winked at Stephanie as they walked down the hall toward the kitchen and living room which were milling about with people that Stephanie both knew and didn't know, voices full of cheer and laughter.

"My dear!" Stephanie's father descended on her quietly from the doorway of the kitchen, giving her a warm embrace and a soft kiss on the cheek.

"Hi, Dad."

Peter Von Feldt aimed a charming and gentle smile at Devon, then extended his hand.

"Pleased to meet you, sir," Devon said smoothly.

"Likewise. I'm Peter."

The pair shook hands in what Stephanie decided was a purely male ritual of communication. They looked each other in the eye and seemed to have a whole conversation while saying absolutely nothing.

"Devon Greene. I appreciate being invited to your beautiful home. This event is talked about all year long and I'm honored to be a part of it."

Stephanie's eyebrow crept up into her hair. She had never seen formal Devon in action. She smiled, knowing that her father was just as casual on the whole as Devon, but watched attentively as the scene played out.

"So nice to hear." Peter released Devon's hand and pulled Stephanie into a one-armed embrace. With a smile painting his lips he glanced from Stephanie to Devon. "Let's cut the bullshit son. You're obviously in love with my daughter, and clearly, she's taken with you. She makes her own rules. As long as you treat her with respect, I've got no qualms with any of that so there's no need to stand on formality. Please, come in, get a drink and some of Mary's amazing food and get comfortable." Peter clapped Devon on the shoulder and turned to greet one of his longtime friends who had just come down the hall.

Devon blinked hard for a moment, stunned into silence. After enjoying his shock for a moment, Stephanie took his hand into hers and started to laugh, breaking the spell.

"Dad likes you." She whispered into his ear as she steered him toward the living room and the banquet tables covered with everything from crudités to bite-sized sandwiches and tiny quiches to slices of cake and pie and partially sliced whole turkeys and hams and all the trimmings.

"That's a relief." Devon visibly relaxed and they both took a glass of champagne.

"You were nervous." Stephanie couldn't help but stare at Devon. She was surprised. Devon Greene was unflappable. She had never considered that he was afraid of meeting her parents. His natural arrogance was an excellent cover for anything resembling fear.

"Of course, I was. I'm living in sin with his baby girl. His only daughter. Never-mind that this is the Von Feldt family we're talking about. From the moment you get an agent in this town, this party is all anyone talks about. If you're lucky enough to come, you've finally made it, to hear some people talk."

Stephanie laughed, ignoring the old tickle of unease that lingered in her mind and navigated them around clusters of people toward the wide sofa she loved so much.

"I haven't heard him put so many words together at one time in years." She sighed, carefully sitting on one of the cushions, taking a sip of her champagne once she was seated.

Devon gave a grin. "Well, I'll take that as a compliment then."

"You should."

Devon, claiming he was too nervous to sit, stood next to Stephanie and sipped at his drink, watching the comings and goings of people.

A huge number of people stopped to say hello to Stephanie, old Hollywood royalty, friends of her parents' that all had something to say about knowing her since she was only 'so big' and complimenting her on what a 'lovely young lady' she had grown up to be.

"You are quite lovely." Devon assured her with a gentle kiss on her temple as she rose to take a bathroom break.

"Thanks. You okay by yourself for a minute?"

"Sure."

Stephanie weaved her way out of sight and headed toward her bedroom to use the bathroom in private.

The space felt quiet and cool to her as she slipped through her childhood room and into the en-suite bathroom. After taking care of her business, she washed her hands and freshened up her makeup and hair.

Before returning to the party she took a wistful look around her room. A fleeting thought about sneaking Devon back here for some private time crossed her mind but she brushed it away with a smile. That would be obvious and still strange in her parents' house. Maybe later she would have an opportunity to show him the pool house, however…

With a genuine warm grin on her lips, Stephanie returned to the giant living room and found Devon in an animated conversation with Marty, Samuel, Maxwell, her father and a couple other older gentlemen she didn't recall the names of.

As they all laughed at Devon's joke, he caught her eye from across the room and smiled. Her heart warmed and she couldn't help but grin back. Love definitely does strange things to you, she decided.

"Seems as though you're getting along fine without me." She said.

"Hey, Kid!" Marty opened his arms for a hug, and Stephanie embraced him happily, laughing as always as he patted her back, awkwardly, his chin barely at her shoulders, especially since she was wearing heels.

Samuel was next for a quick hug, then the group dispersed, off to chat with another group of Hollywood elite. Maxwell threw her a grin and a wink, and she just knew he'd be texting her later on for gossip.

He really hadn't been himself lately and she had yet to truly figure out why. She knew he was struggling with what he wanted to do in his career and Olivia wasn't going away like she should, but her normally bright and shiny friend was unusually dull. That was scary. Hopefully, she'd get it out of him sooner rather than later.

As the hours passed, Stephanie noticed that the party expanded from the immense living space into the dining room, the kitchen, the hallway, even out onto the patio despite the chill in the air.

She said hello to a number of her long-lost former girlfriends and other young actors and actresses who approached her. Devon had wandered off on his own to shake hands, rub shoulders and otherwise mingle with the exceedingly large crowd.

With the help of a team of other women, Mary kept the tables overflowing with food and drink, all of it delicious. Stephanie made a point to find Mary a couple of times, asking if she needed any help.

"Oh, you are the sweetest thing." Mary swept her into a warm hug. "But this is my shining moment for the year and your time to just be at the party. Go dance with your handsome date." Mary winked at Stephanie and shooed her out of the kitchen for the third time.

Devon had managed to nurse just a few beers all day and night, but Stephanie had made the mistake of continuing to drink the fantastic rose champagne her father brought in especially because it was Stephanie's favorite until it was too late.

She stood, then sat right back down again as the world spun.

"Uh oh."

"What's wrong?" Devon's face was pure worry, and Stephanie loved him more for it.

"Too much champagne."

He laughed. "I thought that might happen. Just sit there for a few minutes. I'll go find some water."

Stephanie nodded and looked around the living room. Anyone who was anyone was in her parents' house. Her gaze wandered from reality TV star to soap opera queen to a cluster of animators and composers. As her eyes passed over a familiar face near the drinks table, she could feel the blood leave her face.

At that moment, the man looked up and saw her too.

Feeling as though she might be sick, but afraid to move, Stephanie could only stare as he approached her.

"Steph! How's it going?"

"Hi, Jared." She managed.

"Really? That's all you have to say to me after all these years? *Hi*?" Jared stared at her with his hazel eyes, blonde hair falling into his eyes as he leaned forward slightly to talk to her.

"What do you want me to say, Jared?" Stephanie swallowed over a dry lump in her throat, eyes frantically searching for Devon.

"I don't know, how about, 'Sorry for trashing your career, Jared.'" His eyes flashed with anger and something bordering on violence.

Stephanie continued sitting, trying to remain calm. How had he gotten in here? Where were her parents? Devon? Why wasn't anyone around them paying attention to what was happening? Her throat suddenly felt tight and she could feel the alcohol pounding through her system as the adrenaline dumped into her veins.

"None of that was my fault, Jared, and you know that." The steadiness of her voice didn't let on to her rapidly pounding heart.

He let loose a jaded chuckle, which did finally attract some attention to them. Stephanie put on a pained smile, eyes betraying her near panic.

"None of it is your fault?" Jared's strikingly handsome face contorted into an ugly scowl as he leaned even further toward her, one of his hands clenched into a fist.

"Hate to interrupt, but I don't believe we've met before." Devon inserted himself smoothly between Stephanie and Jared, looking calm on the outside, but Stephanie could see his tension level was through the roof. Devon offered a hand to Jared.

Jared looked pointedly at Devon's outstretched hand and snorted.

"I know who you are. She's a real ball-buster, right? Break it off right at the high point of your year without so much as a backward glance. I saw what she did to you at that premiere. You have my sympathies, brother."

Devon's jaw clenched; icy blue eyes cold for the first time Stephanie could remember.

"I am so not your brother. And what happened was my fault. I was dumb enough to cheat on Stephanie and try to blame her for it. I'm guessing you know the feeling."

The lie came out easily enough. Damn, they had made a mess of things with certain parts of their charade.

Jared growled. Stephanie could see her father and a number of people coming quietly around the crowd of people in the living room.

"I think you've had too much to drink, Jared. What

say we call it a night?" Peter Von Feldt spoke in a soothing tone, treating Jared like a wounded animal that might strike out because of pain or surprise.

Jared turned to look at him and realized that the whole party was watching them.

"No thanks, Peter. I'd rather finish my conversation if you don't mind."

Stephanie had never seen her father like he was at that moment. He was quiet, but in a deadly kind of way.

"No, Jared. As you were not invited to this party to begin with, you will leave. Now. And you will not, under any circumstances, return. Ever."

Jared turned angrily to Stephanie's father, only to be confronted by a number of very strong, very large action movie actors, Alan among them.

"You should go, man." One of them said.

"Yep. Time to leave." Alan gestured to the door, murder painting his features.

"We're not finished!" Jared growled over his shoulder as he was herded out of the room and toward the front door.

"Yes, we are, Jared. Have been for a long time." Stephanie managed, her shoulders sagging in relief, all vestiges of her champagne buzz having evaporated.

Her father asked how she was and she assured him she was okay, all with raised eyebrows and nods. The party quickly resumed around them, talk bubbling up slowly and then feeling overwhelming to Stephanie's ears.

"You alright?" Devon knelt in front of her, his warm hands on her knees.

"I'm okay. Want to get out of here?"

"Thought you'd never ask." He quirked a smile for her, and they made their departure, promising her mother that they would stop by the following day to pick up leftovers and have a quiet brunch.

As they drove through the city toward Devon's condo, Stephanie wished she had a whole bottle of that pink champagne to help her get through what she now felt was necessary to tell Devon about her dating past.

CHAPTER
Twenty-One

STEPHANIE WAS GREETED by a new piece of art-work as they entered Devon's crisp condo.

"When did you get that piece?" She asked, approaching the 3-foot square Alex Felton that was hung above his fireplace.

He smiled broadly.

"Do you like it? I had it commissioned a while back. I just got it delivered a couple of weeks ago. I'm in love with it." He gave a lopsided grin, then swept her up in a quick kiss. "I mean, it's no you, but I love it."

Stephanie nodded. "It's fantastic." And it was. It was one of her very favorite pieces. She had been slowly working through her list of commissions when inspiration had directed this large canvas. It was all light and shadows, primary colors and bold statements, something very unusual for her in general. Her heart was pounding with pride that

Devon was the one who had ended up with it and that he loved it as much as he appeared to.

He eyed her wolfishly and pulled her into an embrace as they regarded the painting. His very touch seemed to make her whole-body stand alert and pay attention. Without speaking, Stephanie tugged him gently toward his bedroom. Devon didn't argue.

After they had shed their party clothes, Devon had taken Stephanie to his bed and in a very slow methodical manner had made love to her. No part of her body had gone unloved, un-worshipped. Every inch of her flesh tingled with pleasure and she was more relaxed than she could ever remember being. It was one of the sweetest nights she'd had in memory, and as they lay in the quiet, tucked into each other's arms, she began to speak.

"I need to tell you about what happened tonight."

"No, you don't." Devon slowly ran his fingers over her spine, his voice rumbling through his chest under her ear.

"Yes, I do."

"Whatever you need Steph. I love you no matter what happened way back when with that douchebag Jared Collins."

Stephanie smiled.

"I know you probably read about it, but we were quite the pair back in the day." She could feel Devon's head nod against the pillows, his hand stilled and was a warm weight against her shoulder-blades. "I was head over heels for Jared Collins, and who wouldn't have been? He was the biggest star on the biggest show on TV." Stephanie found a crack in the ceiling and fixed her gaze on it as she waded through the memories. "I was stupid, and young. And I thought he loved me."

"You were together a pretty long time, right?" Devon's voice was barely above a whisper.

"Yes. Two years."

Devon let out a low whistle. "For those of us that suck at relationships, that's a really long time."

Stephanie couldn't help but chuckle, appreciating that he was trying to bring some levity to the situation. It's just how he was, and she loved him for it. She realized that she loved most things about Devon Greene, and it was a comfort where it should have frightened her.

"I guess. Like I said, we were young. I was 20 when we got involved. I was fairly certain that he and I would get married, have children and live happily ever after." She stopped, and her heart throbbed as she remembered the hurt of their awful drawn-out relationship and the horrible way it had ended.

"What happened, Steph?"

"He didn't realize that I thought dating should be an exclusive thing. He was still seeing any number of my so-called friends on the side."

Devon grunted. He didn't sound surprised.

"Friends?"

Stephanie nodded, moving her eyes from the crack in the ceiling to Devon's strong jawline and aquiline nose.

That silhouette haunted her, no matter how often she painted it.

"Yes. All of my girlfriends, at one point or another. If they didn't get caught or admit it, they vanished altogether which was as good as confessing. Which is why I don't really have any girlfriends. I think Jared managed to sleep with eight or nine of my nearest and dearest. Which I suppose was a good thing—if they were my closest friends and could do that to me, I'm better off without them, right?"

Devon grunted again in agreement, fingers combing through her hair.

"When I would find out about it, he would tell me it wasn't what I thought, that they were just friends too, blah, blah, blah. I bought it. Every time. Even though I knew it wasn't true. I was so scared to lose my happy ending that I let it keep happening."

"When did it start?"

"We had only been together for two months when I found the first pair of panties that didn't belong to me under his bed."

"Oh my god." Devon sat up, and Stephanie was forced to as well. "Seriously? I'm so sorry he did that to you, Steph."

His outrage made his eyes twinkle in a way that should have been anything but adorable and sexy, but Stephanie couldn't help but smile. She kissed his lips softly and he relaxed.

"Yes, he's an idiot, but I didn't leave, either. I thought he loved me, and I thought I loved him, so I stayed. And stayed. And stayed." Stephanie sighed. "I was miserable. I had no friends—well, except Maxwell, I suppose. My boyfriend was a cheater and a liar and I couldn't get a part because I was too large. My early twenties were awful." Stephanie couldn't help but laugh, tears threatening to fall. Devon smiled with her. "Turns out he wasn't ever interested in me. Well, he was, but not as a person. He wanted to use my name, my fame, my status to boost his. And it worked, for a long time. As he said tonight, he still thinks it's my fault that his career tanked after we broke up. He lost his Hollywood royalty girlfriend with the fancy last name and couldn't get any work after his show got canceled."

Devon was quiet, eyebrows drawn together as he watched her.

"There. That's it. The whole ugly mess."

Devon took her mouth in a slow, deliberate kiss. Stephanie couldn't remember her own name when he finally pulled away.

"That's where you got the idea for the business." He said softly, his eyes conveying his sorrow that the basis for her brilliant and successful business idea was rooted in pain and sorrow.

"Yes. And it worked amazingly well."

"So, everyone after Jared…" Devon let his question hang, eyeing her playfully.

Stephanie sighed, finally giving in. She decided in that moment that she didn't care if Devon knew the client list.

If he spilled his guts about it to anyone, she would figure out how to deal with it.

"Everyone after Jared." She said simply.

"Really?" His eyebrows shot up. "Everyone? I would never have believed that. You're good. And that's actually really sad for you. Explains Brett Masterson, though."

They lay back down and Stephanie began to gently trace patterns on his chest.

"It's good to know I had everyone fooled. Brett Masterson… well, I'm not sure what I was thinking with Brett Masterson, but I'm glad it worked out. I was pretty disoriented after our fake breakup." She waited for that admission to sink in, for both of them. Feeling a bit brave, she asked the question she was mentally scolding herself for wanting to ask. "Devon, what's the real truth about you and Nora?"

Devon burst out laughing, but he also grimaced. "I literally just wondered if you were going to ask me that—and well within your rights, to be sure."

Stephanie smiled; his reaction somehow soothing instead of agitating. "I mean, we weren't dating, you and I. We were pretending. We were friends with a business contract and a fake relationship."

"Yes, but it didn't stop me from feeling guilty. I never dated her for real. Not ever. We're not like that at all. But I did double-cross you—I started pretend seeing her a couple of weeks before the breakup at the premiere."

For some unexplainable reason, Stephanie's heart clenched and her eyes filled with hot tears. She tried to rationalize with her brain, that it wasn't actually cheating, but her heart said differently.

Devon glanced over and saw the shimmer in her eyes.

"Oh, Steph. I'm so sorry. I never meant to hurt you." He looked distraught.

Stephanie shook her head and swiped at the tears.

"No, no. It's okay, really. We weren't dating. Not really. Neither were you and her, I get it. I don't know what's wrong with me." But she did. Jared had left a giant hole and she was still trying to convince herself that it had been filled. And it had been, multiple times over.

"I'll make it up to you." He got her favorite devilish grin on his face and swept down with a soul-stealing kiss that left no part of her mouth unexplored. Filled with a sudden need for him, in every way, Stephanie reached for him.

Devon, without removing his mouth from hers, rolled on top of her and used a knee to nudge apart her legs. Stephanie complied, happy to push aside old, bad memories and replace them with the sweet thoughtless desires that seemed to consume her when she was with Devon.

He pushed into her slowly, then with a firm thrust that had Stephanie moaning against his shoulder.

"I love you, Steph." He sighed into her hair as he thrust into her, this time with urgent need, almost as though he were claiming her as his own.

"I love you, Devon." She tilted her body closer to him, wrapping her legs around his waist, teetering on the edge of oblivion as he meshed his flesh with hers in a frantic rhythm.

As she was calling out his name, her body filled with what felt like sparks of electricity, she could feel his generous erection throb an indication of his climax and she fell over the edge, panting and clutching onto him with everything she had.

Afterward, as they lay in a tangle of limbs, unable to speak or move, Stephanie allowed herself to fill with the glow she had denied herself since she dated Jared. She allowed the idea of forever to take root and smiled, thankful that after years of shutting it out it hadn't abandoned her after all.

Twenty-Two

DEVON FOLLOWED STEPHANIE back home after brunch with her parents the following day, and they returned to their predictable routine.

After the Thanksgiving party, the tabloids were abuzz with the revelation that Devon and Stephanie were again an item, and Stephanie had never been so happy to be in Santa Barbara away from the madness.

"I knew they would find out eventually," Stephanie shrugged, turning off the TV. "We'll figure out how to manage it."

With the thousands of people that had come and gone at the party, and Jared's tantrum drawing attention to them, Stephanie wasn't surprised and was in fact shocked at her lack of concern.

"We'll deal with it, babe." Devon smiled reassuringly.

After a quiet New Year celebration between just the two of them, a bottle of champagne and a shocking lack of clothing, Devon woke in the middle of the night to find Stephanie missing from the bed.

As usual, he found her painting.

He stood back for a while, watching her make long brush strokes with navy and midnight blue and violet. She very nearly danced as she directed the paint where she wanted it to go, arms moving broadly as she swept pigment up and down and in directions Devon thought impossible. Still undetected, he moved closer as she switched to plum and magenta and even began to run into Kelly green and shamrock.

Stephanie's whole body jumped as he approached her from behind, his steps startling her out of her painting induced tunnel-vision.

"It's wonderful." He breathed; eyes wide as he took in the massive canvas.

Stephanie blushed and mumbled her thanks.

Devon, looking curious, went even closer to the painting to examine the brushwork. After a few moments, his brow furrowed. Stephanie realized her heart had never slowed down from being startled. She began to put her brushes in the solution for cleaning, scraping her palette free of paint. He'd never examined her artwork closely before. Admired, sure, but never really looked.

"Something the matter?" She asked finally, his scowl having deepened.

He shook his head, still looking at the painting and not at her.

Stephanie just stood and watched him, growing increasingly nervous.

"It can't be." He muttered, turning to look at her. "Is this … I don't … " he seemed to be having trouble forming the sentences he wanted.

Devon strode back to where Stephanie was standing. He looked at the painting from the distance she was away, then back to Stephanie's face. He was dressed only in his favorite linen pants, Stephanie in a tank top and only her panties.

"What?" She asked finally.

He appraised her face, his brightening and splitting into an ear to ear grin.

"You're Alex Felton."

Stephanie said nothing, but he didn't seem to care. His words began to barrel out of him, increasing in volume and enthusiasm as they did so.

"You are. Holy hell. I can't believe it." Devon swept her into his arms and spun her around a couple of times. "Oh God, that explains so much." He planted a feverish kiss hard on her lips and put her down as he started to laugh, relief evident in his posture.

Stephanie smiled. "I never said I was."

"But you have to be! Look at that brushwork! It's the mingling of colors, the way the brush moves through the paint, it's everything I love about the piece I commissioned, it's everything I love about the painting that first caught my attention in the lobby of the Wilshire." He paused. "Stephanie Alexandra Von Felt. Alex Felton. You cagey devil." His playful expression and enthusiasm made Stephanie laugh.

"Just don't tell anyone, okay? I'm doing pretty well with it. Somehow all my jobs are top secret. Why is that?"

"I don't know babe, but I can't believe you're my favorite artist and my favorite girl all in one gorgeous, permanent-vacation package."

Devon punished her mouth with a kiss and then swept her up again, carrying her to the bedroom before she could object. Which really, she couldn't imagine having done anyhow, so who could blame him? He didn't even complain about the multitude of color streaks shared between their skin when all was said and done.

Stephanie realized that she was more than happy. She was content. It was a feeling she thought she'd had before, but clearly, she'd been mistaken. This was a somehow simultaneously floaty and grounded sensation, and she reveled in it. Her concrete box and soap bubble had finally found a way to live in harmony, and her being safe on the inside was completely different than it had ever been before. This was a warm, movable, livable space; not a confining, exclusionary box for protection.

Safe.

Content.

No longer lonely.

SOMEHOW DEVON TALKED Stephanie into coming into Los Angeles for Valentine's Day. Going to dinner anywhere was a total shit-show, and just being out in the general population was certain to be a nightmare.

"It'll be great, I have reservations at Nobu and we'll get to relive our pretend dating days." He begged.

Finally, Stephanie had relented. Orgasms may have been involved.

She went by to see her parents for the day and dressed in the lace peek-a-boo dress that Devon was so very fond of for their date.

"Oh my, darling, that is an incredible dress on you!" Her mother gushed, hands up by her face.

Stephanie could feel the blush in her cheeks.

"Thanks, Mom."

"If I didn't know Devon, and *like* him," Her father growled. "I would forbid you to leave the house in that, no matter how old you are."

"Thanks, Dad." Stephanie hugged her father, who was giving high praise indeed, even though it clearly made him totally uncomfortable.

Stephanie heard her phone chime.

D: *Running behind, can you meet me there? Don't want to lose the reservation. Sorry!*

Stephanie answered that she could do that, and carefully climbed into her Mini Cooper so as not to crumple the dress.

Traffic was indeed a total nightmare, and Stephanie was silently wondering how she had let herself get talked into Valentine's Day dinner out when she finally pulled into the parking lot at the sushi restaurant.

As she allowed the valet to take her car, she steeled herself for the flashbulbs and put on 'the smile' which felt a bit rusty from disuse.

Stephanie felt her heart stutter as she entered the lobby. Devon was kissing Nora on the cheek near the hostess stand.

Feeling possessive and irrationally angry, she strode purposefully in their direction, lots of eyes on her, no doubt because of the dress. Maybe the murderous look on her face had something to do with it too.

Nora saw her coming and put on a bright smile. Devon had the good sense to look a bit nervous.

"Oh hi! So good to see you again Stephanie!" Nora poured on the sugar, air-kissing Stephanie's cheeks.

"You too, Nora."

"Well, I'll see you later, Devon. Have a great night!" Nora swished her narrow hips as she walked away, headed out of the restaurant.

Stephanie couldn't even find words to ask what she wanted to know. She just raised her eyebrow.

Devon smiled at her, then took in the fact that she was wearing the dress.

"Wow. I mean WOW. I do *love* that dress. Shall we?" He placed his hand on the small of her back to guide her.

He left the Nora interaction lying there. Her guts were all tangled up in one another, her mind trying to sort out why she was so upset, what was real and what wasn't and how many layers deep the lies must go. Was she crazy? Why couldn't she accept that they were just friends when she knew that kind of relationship existed? She had one with Maxwell for crying out loud.

Stephanie put on a smile and went with him into the dining room, the hostess leading the way.

She pulled out every acting trick in her arsenal to be sure that Devon didn't feel her suspicions.

Unfortunately, throughout dinner, Stephanie was engaged in a heated mental battle. Surely that was just one friend greeting another? Was Nora the reason Devon was running late? Why would she have been here? Did Nora have her own date? Where was he? Was there something else entirely going on? But Devon would never do that, would he? Not knowing what he did about Stephanie's past and the whole deal with Jared?

She knew she was being irrational, and things were not always anything like they seemed, but her brain was in runaway mode, headed straight toward old wounds and insecurities.

Stephanie forcefully pulled herself into the conversation Devon was admirably trying to keep going, and she really tried to enjoy the fantastic meal.

It was romantic to be sure, no matter what shadows her mind kept trying to cast over the mood.

As they were leaving, Stephanie was beginning to feel silly about suspecting that he and Nora had been up to no good before she got there. Exhausted from the mental tennis match and acting her way through the meal didn't even begin to cover it.

The valets went to retrieve their cars, and Stephanie felt totally blinded by flashbulbs and couldn't seem to block out the flurry of inane questions the photographers were hurling at them. She was completely off balance and hated it.

"Stephanie, do you trust that Devon won't cheat on you with Nora again? Wasn't she here earlier tonight? What do you think about that?"

"Devon, weren't you seen earlier with Nora? Are you dating her or Stephanie?"

"Stephanie, what do you have to say about Jared Collins?"

Finally, the cars arrived.

"Is there a reason that Devon arrived without you, Stephanie? Why would you drive separately to an intimate Valentine's day date?"

The valet opened Stephanie's door, and she slid in, feeling overwhelmed, suspicions once again on high alert, a knot in her gut and in her throat.

Not thinking, she steered her car toward her home and was 30 minutes outside of Los Angeles when her phone chimed.

D: *I'm so sorry about tonight. Are you coming over?*

Stephanie activated the voice to text command.

S: *I don't think so. I was pretty overwhelmed tonight. I'm headed back to my place. I'm sorry.*

She was. This was not at all how she'd predicted their date going.

D: *That's okay. It's my fault. I love you. Be safe.*
S: *Love you too.*

Stephanie's chest tightened and she blinked against the tears. Something about the messages felt final, distant. She drove like the devil was chasing her back to the sanctity of her loft, despair sinking into her bones.

Twenty-Three

STEPHANIE GREW INCREASINGLY tense over the next few days.

After they had parted ways following the uncomfortable dinner date and dealings with the paparazzi, Devon had been strangely quiet.

The first day she chalked up to his shooting schedule, knowing his call sheet—and Nora's—were full, but when she sent a late-night text asking how the shoot went and getting a very short answer, she started to get a cold feeling in her gut. After a second full day of one word or very clipped responses, and going through every scenario possible in her mind Stephanie resorted to calling Marty.

She realized what she was doing was a little silly and maybe a little invasive, but she couldn't shake the feeling that something was genuinely wrong. The sinking, creepy-crawly sensation in her gut had to stop—one way or the other.

Stephanie dialed Marty's number with a fingertip covered in canary yellow and sunburst orange paint.

"Stephanie! My favorite girl, what can I do for you, kid?" Marty enthusiastically answered. Stephanie could hear the tell-tale echo indicating that she was on speakerphone.

"Just wondering if you can pull some strings and get Devon's official schedule for me, Marty. Can you put a feeler out for his set call time this week?"

Marty stayed quiet, then a click indicated he had lifted the receiver instead of leaving her on speaker.

"Sure thing. Any particular reason you're asking?"

Stephanie paused in her pacing and looked at her TV, which had been on but muted for most of the day.

"Just trying to plan a surprise, Marty. Nothing to worry about."

He gave a disbelief covered chortle. "Sure, kid. Whatever you say. I'll email you what I find out."

Stephanie thanked him and hung up. A few minutes later she realized that she didn't need the schedule after all.

Her mind blanked and her hands started to shake as the entertainment reporter silently spoke on her TV screen. The photos were what Stephanie focused on, then a video, both reported to have come from earlier that day.

The photos showed Devon and Nora together at a coffee shop, sitting at a table. That seemed innocent enough, co-workers and friends often have coffee together, and Stephanie was well aware of the fact that Devon and Nora were actively both. There were any number of similar pictures and short videos of her and Maxwell doing exactly the same thing. The footage then showed them leaving the coffee shop.

Through a series of photos on the screen, Stephanie's guts clenched and her heart dropped as she saw them enter a high-end jewelry store and Devon pointed to something in the counter and Nora tried it on. Not earrings, not necklaces. Rings. Diamond rings.

The video was even worse. It showed Devon putting different rings on Nora's slender finger, her smiling and modeling them for him with different gestures, turning her hand so the sparkly gems would catch the light. Stephanie very nearly heaved the contents of her stomach at the cutesy smile Nora was giving Devon. And his enamored expression … oh how Stephanie's heart began to pound in a fractured way when that part of the video played.

The video was heavily edited, condensing what may have been an hour into just seconds of shopping. At the very end, Devon was shown leaving the jewelry store with Nora, kissing her on the temple with an arm around her shoulders, jewelry bag in his hand. There he was, helping Nora into her car—an oddly dated sedan—closing the door and waving goodbye to her before turning a totally out of character glare and an upraised hand to the camera.

Stephanie sat down hard on the sofa and turned the TV off.

Had their whole relationship been a lie? Some kind of game? Had Stephanie Von Feldt been played by Devon Greene? Had she given her heart and body to a man who claimed to love her but never really had?

Sounding as though it were in a tunnel somewhere miles away, Stephanie's phone chimed.

Pulling her thoughts back to something coherent, she got to her feet and located the phone on her kitchen counter. Her heart was pounding, cheeks hot as she read the screen.

D: *I can explain.*

How many thousands of times had her long-ago ex, Jared, used those words? The ex who had been using her for her name, her social status, her face, for crying out loud? How many times had he promised that he really did love her, only to do something very like what she had just seen on the TV screen? She had sworn to herself after those horrible two years that she would never, ever be treated that way again. And the damnedest thing about it was that Stephanie was in love with Devon. She had thought he was the one. Her emotions shifted from despair to anger.

"Not again." She whispered to herself, setting the phone back down on the counter and walking away, swiping at some errant tears on her cheek as she strode purposefully to her bathroom, blasting the shower as hot as she could stand to wash away the hurt.

STEPHANIE'S PHONE CONTINUED to chime at her, call after call from Devon unanswered, texts and voicemails ignored. Finally, she shut the phone off so that it would quit making noise at her.

After her shower, she walked down to the deli and got a sandwich which she didn't really eat, and ran through every possible scenario while sitting on the beach watching the waves crash against the shore.

Her whole body hurt, her heart ached and her head was pounding. Stephanie was with it enough to notice that she felt entirely too calm. She was miserable, for sure, but part of her just couldn't believe that the last six months had been a ruse. Nobody was that good.

Weren't they though?

Because *she* was.

She was that good, and why couldn't he be too? She'd given him all her best tips and insider tricks when he'd been a client.

She'd given him her everything.

A quiet cold stole over her as the sun dipped below the horizon. Gathering her trash and mostly-uneaten sandwich, she slowly walked back to her apartment.

Her body felt so weak she had a difficult time drag-ging herself up the stairs. Once the door was safely locked behind her, she allowed herself to collapse into bed, no matter the early hour. Tears came hot and wet and violent as she moaned into her pillow, chest aching as though her heart had been torn from it.

She agreed to listen to the messages in the morning, but for that night she was allowing herself to grieve.

I can explain.
It's not what you think.
Please answer me.
Stephanie, I love you, I swear there's nothing going on between Nora and me.
I know how it looked, but I promise there's a good explanation.
Stephanie, please, I love you.

STEPHANIE FELT A hot stab every time she hit the delete button on one of Devon's messages. She wanted to believe him, wanted to talk to him but didn't trust herself. Jared had managed to con her for nearly two years. She wouldn't be made a fool of like that again.

The phone vibrated in her hand. It was her father. This was his second attempt to reach her. Maxwell had tried half a dozen times. It wouldn't surprise her if Max showed up at her door, honestly.

Maybe she wanted him to.

For a moment, Stephanie debated ignoring her father's call. He so rarely called though, what if something was wrong with him or her mother?

"Hi, Dad." She tried to sound cheerful but knew she fell way short.

"Hi, Honey. Are you alright?"

Stephanie sighed and fought against the tears in her eyes.

"I'll be okay, Dad."

Stephanie could hear her father let out a heavy breath.

"Listen, Stephanie, you know how the tabloids are. Have you talked to Devon?"

Stephanie felt a stab of anger.

"No, Dad, I haven't. How in the world could they be inventing the fact that he was ring shopping with another woman?"

"I didn't say anything of the sort. Have you spoken to him? Let him tell you what really happened?"

She sat on the bench at the dining room table.

"No."

"Stephanie Alexandra." He admonished, the tone of his voice making her shrink into herself just like it had when she was a child. The power of the full name was pretty incredible. "You know better than to make rash decisions based on what the entertainment media puts on television, on in a paper, or online."

Stephanie found herself inexplicably smiling. It was a rare occasion that her father scolded her, and while she did feel her cheeks flame in shame, it was exactly what she needed in that moment.

"I do know that. Thanks for the reminder, Dad."

"Wait. Thanks?" Her father faltered as he prepared to further argue with her.

"Yes. I'll talk to him. I just…was remembering Jared and how awful that was."

Her father chuckled, then sighed.

"I remember how badly you were hurt over Jared, Stephanie. Let me assure you that Devon is not Jared, never could be. He even charmed Marty. And *Alan* for goodness sake."

Stephanie felt a raw chuckle bubble up out of her throat.

"You're right Dad. I love you. Kiss Mom for me?"

"Of course, darling. Feel free to call or come by if you need anything. We miss you."

Stephanie and her father exchanged their love and she hung up, more confused than before.

Maxwell took that opportunity to text her as well. One simple message that said:

Don't be an idiot. Think this through.

She wasn't sure exactly which direction he was trying to push her, to be honest.

She was startled by the whirring sound of her dumb-waiter activating on its own. Stephanie padded into the kitchen and stood in front of the counter, watching as it returned. Once it was fully docked, she opened the door and found a note.

Please, let me explain. I promise it's nothing like you think.—Devon

War raged inside Stephanie's body for a moment. Her father's words rang in her ears, her desire to believe Devon and have everything be alright winning over.

She scribbled "meet me on the patio" on the back of the note and went to change into a clean dress and find some shoes, moving before she could have second thoughts.

Less than 2 minutes later, Stephanie opened her door to find Devon sitting on the floor just outside her door.

He looked terrible, eyes red-rimmed and hair dishev-eled. His clothing was rumpled as though he had slept in them, maybe multiple times. His icy blue eyes gave the slightest twinkle as he looked at her.

"Can I come in? Please?" Those magnificent blue wells shimmered with hope and fear.

Stephanie had wanted to be in a public place, but nod-ded and moved back to allow him space to come in. Devon jumped to his feet and scurried into her apartment before she could change her mind.

Arms crossed over her chest, Stephanie appraised him with her eyes. Devon ran a hand through his hair, making it stand on end just a little bit more, and then began to gesture widely as he spoke.

"I know how it looked. Really, I do. That was beyond stupid."

Stephanie just raised an eyebrow, heart pounding. Being in his presence was nearly intoxicating. She loved him, she really did and with every fiber of her being. It was difficult to keep from running to him, believing him, but she tried to maintain with her heavy measure of doubt.

"We did go in together; we did shop together. Tell me though, Stephanie, you saw the photos. You saw the video. Which one of us left with the bag?"

Stephanie felt her brows knit together.

"I don't understand."

"Think about what you saw." Devon came close and looked into her eyes imploringly. "Who left the store with the bag?"

Stephanie studied his handsome face as her memory tried to pin down the answer to what he was asking her. She felt her eyes widen as the answer surfaced.

"You did." She could barely whisper it. The amount of stupidity she felt at that moment was crushing.

Devon smiled and nodded.

"You could have handed it to her when she got in the

car." Stephanie was feeling like an idiot, scrambling for further explanations.

"Nope." His face broke into a smile. He knew he had her. Devon gently held her face in his hands and planted a soft, slow kiss on her mouth. All the fight left Stephanie's body. She gave herself over to the kiss, and the fact that Devon wasn't lying, wasn't having an affair, wasn't in love with anyone but her.

She was an idiot.

Shame swamped her body as she realized that she had allowed all the cuts Jared had made to bleed all over Devon.

For a moment after the kiss broke, Stephanie stole a glance at Devon, then put her hands over her eyes as if to hide.

"I'm sorry, Devon. I assumed the worst. I just saw… Well, you know what I saw."

"Open your eyes, babe."

Stephanie removed her hands and opened her eyes. Her gaze adjusted and her heart skipped. Devon was no longer standing in front of her, rather he was down on one knee in front of her, the most spectacular ring she had ever seen extended to her.

"Stephanie Von Feldt, or Alex Felton, whoever you really are," he smirked and she found herself smiling, tears filling her eyes. "Would you do me the most incredible honor of being my wife? I can't imagine spending any significant amount of time without you. I may do vacations and relationships wrong, but nothing else in the whole world has ever felt this right. Marry me? Please?"

Tears overwhelmed Stephanie's eyes, but they felt very different than the ones that had been full of sorrow. They were warm and soft, whereas the ones fueled by anger were prickly and hot.

"Yes." She felt the word come out of her. Again, with actual intention, her voice worked around the word. "Yes."

Devon rose and wrapped his arms around her. She found herself warm and full of lightness.

"I'm so sorry I doubted you." She mumbled into his shoulder.

"I'm sorry I was dumb enough to go about this in a way that would cause you to doubt me."

He planted a breath-stealing kiss on her lips and then pulled away, slipping the cool metal band on her finger.

"It's beautiful."

"I've been looking for quite a while." They adjourned to one of the couches, where Stephanie admired the ring. It was a simple marquis cut, not overly large. There were complementary stones on either side. It was lovely. "I called your parents nearly two months ago. Maxwell nearly three."

"Seriously?" Stephanie could feel her mouth hanging open. "No wonder my mother's been avoiding me. She's terrible with those kinds of secrets! And that's at least part of what's been wrong with Maxwell." At the very least, certain things in her world suddenly made sense.

Devon laughed. "Your Dad was actually really great about it."

Stephanie leaned her head on his shoulder and just took a moment to breathe, feeling complete and buoyant and happy.

"What do you know—turns out you're not so bad at vacation or relationships after all."

"Seems I have you to thank for that," Devon grinned. "I'm only good at them when you're involved."

He smiled at her, that dashing smile she knew she would never get tired of, and planted a sweet kiss on her mouth that reminded her again that he was her match, and she could love him just like this forever.

STEPHANIE AND DEVON were enjoying a beer on the patio of O'Malley's about a week later, Stephanie busy flipping through the mail she had retrieved on their way down.

"Hmm." She furrowed her brow and opened a pink envelope to find a very sweet greeting card from Nora. It included a note of apology for her part in making it appear as though Devon were stepping out on Stephanie, and a few words expressing that she hoped there would be no hard feelings. "That was nice of her," Stephanie mumbled, handing the card to Devon for him to read. "I owe her one—at least one—for when we were pretend dating. That's a big conversation we need to have with her, too."

He nodded his agreement, his dark eyebrows raised in surprise as he read it, and he handed the card back to her with a smile.

"She's really sweet. Good people. There's a reason she's still my friend. But I promise I will let you know when she and I plan to spend time together in case the paparazzi decide to try and spin it the wrong way."

"I appreciate that. The same goes for my friend dates with Maxwell." Stephanie smiled and took a sip of her beer.

Devon leaned across the table and took her hands into his.

"What would you say to an actual vacation?" He asked.

"Like we go away somewhere else?" she teased. "Are you sure you are good enough at vacation at this point to actually take a week and leave the city? Or—gasp—the state?"

He smiled. "Absolutely. Let's go. Anywhere you want."

Stephanie thought. "What about the mountains? I've always wanted to see Colorado."

Devon gave her his heart-melting, knee-weakening grin. "Done."

"Really? That easy?"

Devon laughed and placed a soft kiss in her palm.

"For you, anything. I love you, Stephanie Von Feldt. Let's take a vacation to the mountains."

Stephanie smiled and turned her gaze to her beach. Yes, the mountains would indeed be a welcome change of scenery, no matter how much she adored her ocean.

For the first time, she felt complete and stable and free, and she had Devon to thank. Who would have guessed that being a fake girlfriend could turn into true love?

Epilogue

TO SAY THE wedding was beautiful would be an understatement. It was the perfect balance of beach simplicity and Hollywood elegance.

Marlowe Von Feldt had called in numerous favors, spared no expense and poured herself enthusiastically into the task of planning her daughter's wedding.

Devon's mother had flown out to spend a number of days with Marlowe as well in the months leading up to the nuptials, helping iron out details and pick tablecloths and flowers and all the lovely details that neither Devon nor Stephanie really cared to bother with.

"I just need you, at the altar saying that you will keep me around for a long time. That's all." Devon had teased Stephanie one afternoon as they watched their mothers going over what seemed like hundreds of invitation options at the Von Feldt's dining room table.

"A 'long time'? You're stuck with me permanently, Mr. Greene. Or did you not understand the language in the contract again?" Stephanie had leaned in for a kiss and felt herself falling into the comfort that was Devon's embrace and the warm love they had found for one another.

Every item was perfect. The candles in the centerpieces on the tables, the gauzy bunting flowing in the sea breeze above the arch that led down the aisle. The clean-lined ivory Vera Wang dress, the one item Stephanie had chosen for herself, was matched with the sand tone linen suit that Devon was wearing. His ivory shirt mirrored her gown and his pocket square was the same color as his eyes, which were the same color as the accents and piping on her gown as well as the lilies and orchids in her bouquet.

Neither of them wore shoes.

Perfect.

The event was held on a private strip of Malibu beach that Samuel had donated for the event. The weather was perfect, as June in Malibu is apt to be, and the sunset ceremony was devastatingly gorgeous.

Marlowe had put together a guest list that was somehow perfectly balanced and still shockingly packed full of A-list celebrities.

Hands pressed together up near her face as she watched Stephanie do one final adjustment on her headband of small blue flowers, Marlowe gushed to her daughter.

"Just so perfect. So beautiful. You and Devon are just the best match, darling. You will have a long and happy life together, I just know it."

Stephanie felt tears prickle in her eyes. The approval pouring out of Marlowe was a balm that she hadn't realized she'd needed and craved.

"Thanks, Mom. You've truly outdone yourself. This is all just amazing. And perfect."

The pair shared a hug, and then the music started, signaling that it was Peter's turn to hug his daughter and then take her arm to guide her down the aisle.

Stephanie strode past the rows of white folding chairs full of friends and family and toward her future. Devon was giving her that devilish half-smile she adored, and looked good enough to eat with his hair blowing softly in the sea breeze.

Peter let her go at the altar, and she graced his cheek with a soft kiss.

Maxwell tossed her a wink from his spot as Man of Honor. Across the aisle from him were Devon's three brothers—Dennis, Daniel, and Dallas—all of them very obviously part of the same gene pool. Devon's father, Frank, had very clearly passed along his genes in a copy/ paste manner as they all took directly after him. Except the eyes—those crystalline blue orbs were all Devon's mom, Shelley.

Devon's family had all been nothing but gracious and lovely to Stephanie, and she couldn't be happier about gaining the family she was. She only wished that Alabama was a bit closer so they might have a chance to see one another more often. Guilt about not making an effort to meet them before the actual wedding was something she was going to have to work through, and she felt like that would just take some face time.

"We are here today to join Stephanie and Devon in the bonds of matrimony…" The officiant was a longtime friend of Peter's and had a great big booming voice and spectacular sense of humor. Stephanie had been quite amused by some of the lighthearted aspects of the ceremonial wording, but couldn't focus on anything he was saying as she stared into the depths of Devon's eyes, their hands joined and symbolically tied together with blue ribbon.

"At this time, the couple would like to recite their own vows."

Devon shifted his weight in the sand and looked at Stephanie, a rare look of seriousness on his face.

"Stephanie Von Feldt, I love you more than I could have ever thought possible. I want to be by your side for the rest of my days, no matter where in the world that happens to be, or how many cameras are around, or how many colors of paint you have all over yourself. So, do you, Stephanie, take me as I am, for better or worse, for famous or common, as long as you can possibly stand it?" The crowd tittered and Stephanie smiled brightly at her groom.

"I do." Stephanie paused, glancing at her feet before proceeding with her own vows. "Devon Greene, you are the sunshine in my days and the waves in my ocean. I want to be at your side always, no matter how difficult that might get sometimes with all of the girls throwing themselves at your feet. Do you, Devon, take me as I am, for richer or poorer, for happy or irritable, as long as I want you around?" More laughter.

"I absolutely do."

"Then by the power vested in me, by the state of California, I now pronounce you husband and wife. You may kiss your bride." The officiant gave an adorably lewd wink at Devon.

Devon swept Stephanie up in a sweet but lingering kiss, the crowd cheering as he did so. Once they broke, still beaming at one another, Devon led her back down the aisle and toward the enormous tents where the reception was being held.

"I love you." Stephanie whispered into his ear as they found their seats and the rest of the guests filtered in.

He smiled back at her and kissed her hand so gently it almost tickled, but the rest of her body responded to the gesture in a way that had her nearly moaning in her seat. The look on his face told her that he knew exactly what he was doing to her.

"It's going to be entirely too many hours until I can get you out of that dress."

Stephanie laughed and kissed him again, the party commencing all around them as they enjoyed their first moments as Mrs. And Mr. Greene.

THEY MADE THEIR escape as soon as they possibly could without being totally insulting to their guests. The food had been decadent and spectacular, and Stephanie had danced with every important man in her life until she simply couldn't take wearing her shoes anymore—no offense to Mr. Choo, but she was in pain and they had to go.

Alan, Marty, Samuel, Maxwell and of course her dad had all taken their turns cutting in on Devon. His brothers did so in turns as well, getting a laugh out of her and some playful growling out of him. They were all very sweet and she could only hope she remembered the stories they decided to tell her about their beloved brother later on.

Stephanie was riding a high of her favorite pink champagne and true happiness when they finally tucked themselves into the waiting limo and directed it away from the reception.

Instead of heading back to either Los Angeles or Santa Barbara, they caught a plane headed east.

"Not at all how I pictured taking my wife to bed the first time, but I'll take it." Devon smiled at her wolfishly, carrying her carefully bridal style toward the rear of the private jet.

There were certain perks of celebrity and money, and having access to a full bedroom on a plane was definitely one of them.

She had changed out of her wedding dress and either her mother or Devon's would likely take care of having it preserved while they were gone. Devon had pouted about not getting to be the one to take it off of her, but the simple slip dress she'd traded it for seemed to make him happy enough.

"I've never been in an airplane bedroom." He admitted, kissing his way down her collarbone as he slid the satin off her shoulders.

"Mmm." Was the only semblance of thought she could vocalize.

There was really no time to gather her wits either, because he was kissing the absolute life out of her and guiding her toward the bed before she realized that she was naked.

"Mmm, indeed." He confirmed, stripping himself with nearly as much stealth and speed as he had her.

Stephanie allowed her mind to turn off. Everything was sensation and touch and breath as they explored and felt and embraced one another. On a groan muffled by her neck, Devon pushed inside her, and she pressed back into him. They rocked together in a slow rhythm, no cares in the world except being and feeling.

Their bodies moved together, and Stephanie could feel her climax building clear into her toes. Devon seemed similarly affected by the sounds he was making and the hitch in his smooth pulses. She met his gaze, holding his crystalline eyes, and they locked fingers, his hands guiding hers above her head. A few desperate, deep thrusts later, they moaned into one another's mouths in pleasure and collapsed side by side into the bed.

"I've never had sex with my wife in an airplane bedroom before." Devon teased, breath hot on her neck, their arms and legs still tangled together in the sheets.

"I'd sure hope not. We'd be having a pretty serious conversation about that if you had."

She felt his smile against the skin of her neck and drifted into sleep.

THE PILOT'S INITIAL descent announcement woke them both, and Stephanie quickly set about dressing and gathering their things. Instead of flying into the larger airport, they had chosen a more nearby municipal strip. Hopefully, that meant they would avoid traffic, shorten the time they needed to travel by car and hopefully miss being recognized by more than a handful of people.

Stephanie immediately felt the difference in oxygen levels but the brisk air was welcome, the navy and violet peaks a glorious change of scenery, the sky a very particular and vibrant shade of blue. The temperature was mild, and Stephanie immediately formed a positive affinity for Colorado.

It was a good halfway point between California and Alabama—maybe there was something that could be done to make it the family vacation spot so everyone could get away and yet they could all spend time together. She mentally flagged that thought as something she definitely wanted to revisit.

It was only a short drive to their rented cabin, and Devon managed to charm the agents at the tiny airport rental counter with his endearing smirk and a couple of autographs.

Before she knew it, they were safely within the log walls, a gas fire going for ambiance (it was still June after all) and relaxation sinking into her body, making muscles unknot and joints loosen.

"See?" She teased her new husband, who was curled up with her on the large dark leather couch. "Vacation when done right is amazing."

Devon just smiled at her, planted a gentle kiss on her lips and said, "I told you before—your permanent vacation is really awesome. I'm just glad you're going to let me take it with you."

What girl wouldn't swoon at that? Especially while looking out the window at endless forest, a rippling azure lake and complete serenity?

Stephanie snuggled into his arms and just allowed herself to feel—comfortable, safe, cared for. It was the best feeling in the world.

She knew with absolute surety that taking a chance on Devon and opening herself back up to the possibility of real relationships had been her very own image adjustment, and she had zero regrets.

"Hey, Mrs. Greene?"

"Yes, Mr. Greene?"

"Wife?"

"Husband?"

"Nothing, I just wanted to practice saying 'Mrs. Greene' and 'wife'."

Stephanie shook her head and then laid it on his shoulder. A girl could get used to a whole lot of this. Three weeks seemed like a reasonable head start.

She'd take it. And every other day Devon would give her. A smile rose gently to her lips and she realized that the teacher had become the student—she may have adjusted his image, but he'd taught her to trust and open up to real relationships again—something she had once thought was impossible.

"Well played Mr. Greene." She mumbled, smiling as they snuggled and gazed into the fire. "Well played indeed."

What's next for Nora and Maxwell? Find out in

IMAGE

Protector

Nothing in Hollywood stays a secret for
long, and there's plenty of film that could
destroy everything she's worked for.

NORA CHASE IS a good girl. Her carefully cultivated
public persona is under lock and key – the price
to keep it that way has been steep. Minding her
image at every turn is a small price to pay to continue her
reign as the sweetheart of the small screen. Unfortunately
for Nora, her emotions pay no attention to the moratorium
she's put on relationships where Maxwell, an acquaintance
through mutual friends, is involved.

Maxwell Caine is an entertainment attorney at the
top of his game at one of the biggest firms in town. He's
just not sure that law is where he's actually meant to be.
Temptation to overhaul everything he knows walks into
his conference room one day, and her name is Nora. Falling
for her may be the final push he needs to leave the law

behind and chase his own dreams. He can tell she's hiding something big, however, and she won't let him get close enough to help her.

Maxwell's steadfast presence gives Nora comfort she didn't know she was seeking and isn't sure she deserves. Nora is everything Maxwell didn't know he was looking for. They're a perfect match – but can he stand by her when her past is exposed?

Image Protector is a standalone contemporary Hollywood romance. If you like red hot chemistry, a guaranteed Happily Ever After and a dash of suspense then you'll love this steamy beach read!

continue reading for a sneak peek

AN INDELICATE SQUEAK of surprise left Nora's throat as she flailed and jumped to her feet. Sand and saltwater went flying out from underneath her as she scrambled, legs tangling a bit in the skirt of her bridesmaid's dress.

A cold, gritty, *wet* nose had pressed into her ear, giving her the startle of a lifetime as she gazed out at the Pacific Ocean. The vast expanse of vibrant orange and gold meeting the azure sky had absorbed her attention completely.

She hadn't even heard the massive dog approach over the steady, heavy heartbeat of the waves and now, he was all lolling tongue and happy panting as he gave her a waist hug with his front legs.

"Rufus! Down!"

A familiar man bounded toward them, panic on his incredibly handsome face. Brown eyes wide, he held out a hand as if to stop his dog from accosting her, but it was already too late.

She recognized him; he was her best friend Devon's brand-new wife's best friend. Stephanie was *her* good friend as well, and he'd come up in conversation more than once. His name was Maxwell if memory served.

They'd been in close proximity many times, but never actually met or spoken without a bunch of distractions, and today, having been Stephanie and Devon's wedding day, had been no different.

"I'm so sorry!" He looked horror-struck at the sandy paw prints his dog had left on Nora's plum-colored bridesmaid dress. "He got away from me for just a second-"

"It's okay," Nora brushed the mostly dry sand off her dress and patted the giant mastiff's head once he dismounted her waist and stood between them just happily panting. She couldn't help but smile at the big goofy face. "He didn't hurt me. Just a little surprised is all."

Maxwell visibly relaxed and ran a hand through his light brown hair. He was still in his wedding attire as well, though missing a few pieces. His suit had been pared down to just dress slacks and white button-down shirt, the cuffs of both rolled up. His feet were bare in the sand, his ankles, a bit of collarbone and tanned forearms exposed.

"Sorry again. I know we've met before—I'd know your lovely smile anywhere, in fact—but I'm Maxwell Caine." He extended a hand to her.

"Nora Chase," she replied, shaking his outstretched hand. Her brain registered that the skin was slightly rough but warm.

"Pleased to meet you again, Nora. We were down the table a bit at the rehearsal dinner and on opposite sides of the altar at the wedding." It wasn't a question, though his grin was teasing.

Nora nodded. "Yes. Friend of both the bride and groom, but the groom in particular."

"Me too. But the opposite. How is it we've never really connected before now?" The question lingered between them, Nora giving a slight shrug. His head inclined to the left, adorably.

At the momentary silence, her eyes trailed off to the rolling ocean for a moment, then back to the reception a bit further down the beach under tents strung with twinkly lights.

Her friends were in there, and their families. They were dancing and toasting and happy. The smile pushed at her mouth, and she finally looked away.

The cool ocean breeze tried to whip some of the blonde hair that had escaped her fancy up-do into circles, and she pushed it away from her face.

Maxwell's gaze hadn't once left her face.

"Nothing quite like bending the wedding rules. I love that I was a groom's maid and you were a bride's man."

His laugh was warm and rolled across her skin very pleasantly. The way his expressive eyes appraised her made her feel things she couldn't adequately process. It was nice. And it was dangerous.

"I was Man of *Honor*, thanks very much, but yes, I agree," he paused, chocolate eyes twinkling as he dipped his head to one side again, a playful smile on his lips. "I had to give Rufus here a stroll so I have an excuse. Why aren't you over there celebrating?"

"I needed a breath of air." She couldn't help but return his grin, Rufus panting in devoted adoration of his master, still planted firmly on the sand between them, though he'd given up standing and had taken a seat.

It seemed that the breath caught in her chest as she looked at Maxwell. His gaze communicated attraction, but in the friendliest of ways.

"At an outdoor beach wedding?" he teased, but then nodded gently. "Honestly, I understand that. Well, I'll leave you to it. Maybe I'll see you later? A glass of champagne, perhaps a dance?"

"Sure."

Nora watched one of the most handsome men she had ever met stride back past the party tents and toward the enormous house up above. She wanted to call him back but realized she didn't have the first clue of what she'd say if she did.

She didn't have these kinds of feelings about men. Hadn't since her last boyfriend, a miserable specimen that she wished she could go back and never meet in the first place. There was no time for dating or relationships between her job and the mess back home that was a feud of sorts between her frustrating, needy mother and independent, lovely sister.

Her fingers twitched, knowing the pile of text messages was still waiting for her. Nora had pointedly left her purse safe with the mother of the groom in the party tent. Her mother would not ruin this day with her insistent attempts at getting in touch with her.

Nora took a deep breath and forced those thoughts away, focusing on the man and his dog instead.

Rufus followed Maxwell at a trot, panting and drooling all over the place. A spot in Nora's chest that had been cold warmed as she watched them wander toward the massive house at the edge of the sand. Her reaction to him worried her a bit, but she couldn't resist the urge to welcome it.

Had it not been for some poor choices earlier in her career she wouldn't feel this way, but that was then and this was now.

Rubbing her hands together to clear some stray grains of black and gold Malibu beach sand, she turned her feet back toward the wedding tent, a genuine smile on her face. Yes, she definitely wanted to see more of Maxwell Caine.

That, too, worried her, but she couldn't quite make herself care.

Available NOW at Amazon
and other major book retailers!

"ONE OF THE first steps into true recovery is making amends with those you have hurt or wronged."

The perky, well-spoken therapist was the embodiment of everything Olivia hated about rehab.

She didn't even belong there for starters. There was nothing wrong with her—she wasn't addicted to drugs or alcohol. There were no anger management issues. Sure, she'd made some bad decisions when it came to men, but she wasn't a damn junkie.

If it weren't a condition of her probation for the unfortunate sex-tape debacle she couldn't quite bring herself to regret, she wouldn't even be there. Not for a second.

Her eyes met the aqua ones of a man she recognized across the circle of chairs.

Unable to stop herself, she winked at him.

Ollie Parkinson.

Now there was someone who *should* be in rehab. Olivia had heard all the terrible stories about him floating around; everyone had.

"Olivia? Is there something you'd perhaps like to share today?" The pretty enough therapist smiled at her, and Olivia felt the urge to claw her eyes out of her skull rise suddenly. Intentionally folding her hands in her lap, she appraised the doctor. She was brunette but reminded her enough of that bitch Nora that Maxwell was still seeing that it made her blood rush.

"No, thanks."

The therapist's face dropped a bit, but she recovered quickly.

"That's alright. Sharing is never mandatory, but it can really help the process. Maybe next session."

Olivia felt her face form a pretend smile that she hoped came across the same as if she'd flipped Dr. Feelgood the bird.

After the painfully long feelings-sharing session finally ended, Ollie boldly approached her before she could slip out of the meeting space and return to her tiny cell of a room.

"Hey, Olivia, right?"

"Yeah," she snapped, not trying one bit to mask her impatience.

"Look, I know we don't know one another, but I think we have some … acquaintances in common. I've been here for a few weeks, and I can tell you that it gets easier." He seemed genuine, and for some reason that was worse than him propositioning her like she'd thought he might.

"Okay. Thanks."

He ran a hand through his sandy hair. There was no denying he was handsome, but Olivia wasn't interested. See? Who needed rehab for sex addiction? Not her. She was fine. There was nothing wrong with her at all.

"You want to grab something to eat?" Ollie deployed what should have been a very charming lopsided grin.

"Pass," Olivia said, pushing her way past him and out into the hallway.

"If you need anything..." he trailed off behind her.

"Sure," she said, glancing over her shoulder as her feet carried her quickly down the hall toward her room.

As if.

She was here to do her time and get the hell out, not make friends with the likes of Ollie Parkinson.

Image Destroyer, third and final book in the Image series will provide redemption for these villains in 2021!

Winter BLOOM

**BEST FRIENDS.
ONE WEEK.
A ROAD-TRIP THAT
COULD CHANGE EVERYTHING.**

Phae is ready to hit the road and find herself somewhere along the highway. There's a new life waiting for her in Santa Barbara and she'd love to be there by Christmas. Her original plan was to make the drive solo, but her best friend Daniel has other plans.

Daniel has been totally captivated by his friend Phae since they first met. When he hears that she's planning to drive cross-country alone, he can't help but invite himself along. She'd never stop to smell any of the metaphorical roses without a nudge from him, and distance is about to be a big issue.

Stuck in close-quarters, they are confronted with the notion that they might be meant for more than just friendship. Will their bond survive all the big life changes happening at once or will their relationship become a casualty of the move?

A NOTE FROM *The Author*

THIS BOOK HAS been a *very* long time in the making. Stephanie and Devon came to me quite literally in a dream. I had a very vague idea of a woman who acted her way through relationships as a business and the Image Adjuster was born. I hope you loved reading their story as much as I loved discovering it!

I owe a massive thank you, hug and baked goods to everyone who read it early, late, and everywhere in the middle. You helped mold this book into the story it has become. To my accidental Beta team: Don, Glenn, Lea-Ann, Alley, Jessica, Rhianna, Christopher—this story wouldn't have happened if not for you! For the friends I've never met in person but who still helped me more than I can express (I'm looking at *you*, Shannon Myers) you're the frosting on my cupcake! Seriously. THANK YOU.

If you loved the book I'd really appreciate if you could take just a minute to leave a review. Reviews help both authors and readers!

ABOUT
The Author

ILY IS A Colorado native enjoying the fantastic climate of Southern California with her family and cranky cat after surviving more than a decade in hot, humid places where hurricanes get their own season and Winter is a myth.

The written word is her favorite thing—reading or writing, she doesn't discriminate. Left to her own devices she can read about a book a day; that HEA is a powerful drug!

As an only child she grew up inventing elaborate stories for her dolls to act out. She started word processing on a computer around age 10 and never looked back. After suffering the heartbreak of catastrophic drive failure a regrettable number of times, she has finally learned to back things up appropriately and often.

Follow her antics on social media! (If she disappears for a bit around late August, don't worry, that's just her wanderlust kicking in. She'll be back soon.)

NEWSLETTER:
http://bit.ly/ALANewsletter

WEBSITE:
http://www.authorlilyalexander.com/

FACEBOOK:
http://bit.ly/LilyAlexFB or
https://bit.ly/LilysReaderLounge

BOOKBUB:
https://bit.ly/IPBookBub

INSTAGRAM:
http://bit.ly/ALAInstagram

TWITTER:
http://bit.ly/ALAtwitter

GOODREADS:
http://bit.ly/ALAGoodreads